The
RUNAWAY

Other books by Bernice Thurman Hunter

Booky: A Trilogy
      That Scatterbrain Booky
      With Love From Booky
      As Ever, Booky
A Place for Margaret
Margaret in the Middle
Margaret on Her Way
Lamplighter
The Railroader
The Firefighter
Hawk and Stretch
Amy's Promise
Janey's Choice
Two Much Alike

The RUNAWAY

**Bernice Thurman
Hunter**

Cover illustration by
Tony Meers

Scholastic Canada Ltd.
Toronto New York London Auckland Sydney
Mexico City New Delhi Hong Kong

Scholastic Canada Ltd.
175 Hillmount Rd., Markham, Ontario, Canada L6C 1Z7

Scholastic Inc.
555 Broadway, New York NY 10012, USA

Scholastic Australia Pty Limited
PO Box 579, Gosford, NSW 2250, Australia

Scholastic New Zealand Ltd.
Private Bag 94407, Greenmount, Auckland, New Zealand

Scholastic Publications Ltd.
Villiers House, Clarendon Avenue, Leamington Spa,
Warwickshire CV32 5PR, UK

National Library of Canada Cataloguing in Publication Data
Hunter, Bernice Thurman
  The runaway
ISBN 0-439-98895-0
I. Title.
PS8565.U577R86 2001   jC813'.54   C2001-930476-5
PZ7.H86Ru 2001

Photo on page 121 courtesy Syd Sharp, from *Black Boots and Short Trousers;* all other photos courtesy Neville Robertson.

6 5 4 3 2 1   Printed in Canada   1 2 3 4 5/0

With love and thanks to my son-in-law, Joe Farley,
for his unfailing support through the years,

and

to Neville and Jean Robertson,
for sharing their time and memories.

Contents

1. Runaway 1
2. The First Search 8
3. Memories 12
4. Inquiries 16
5. The Second Search 22
6. The Escort 33
7. The New Boy 39
8. Pocket Money 44
9. Visit to Ipswich 55
10. The Third Search 60
11. Matthew 65
12. Miss Featherstone's House 69
13. The Promise 74
14. Hooligans 78
15. Punishment Postponed 85
16. The Middle of the Night 88
17. The New Boy 92
18. The Magistrate 100
19. Greystone 109
20. Initiation 114
21. Sunday at Greystone 118
22. Homesick 125
23. Christmas at Greystone 130
24. New Year's 134
25. Chores 139
26. Searching Again 146
27. Confessions 150
28. Never Give Up 150
29. The Quest Ends 154

Chapter 1

Runaway

"Graham Robbertson!" Mother Button's sharp tongue stopped him in his tracks.

"Yes, Mother?" Mother Button wasn't really his mother, but that's what she liked the boys to call her.

"You nicked my sweet coupons." It was 1946 and the war was over, but sweets were still rationed in England. Mother Button held the empty coupon box upside down and gave it a good hard shake. "What did you do with them?" she demanded.

"Nothing. I didn't steal nothing." He didn't know what she was talking about.

"Don't lie to me, Graham Robbertson. You were seen taking them."

"Who seen me? Whoever said that is a bloomin' liar."

"Mind your tongue, young man." She thumped the lid back on the empty box. "Watt's Sweetshop just got an order of humbugs in today and I can't buy them without my coupons. Off you go to school now. And it's straight to bed for you tonight with no supper. And if you don't bring those coupons home with you, you needn't come home at all!" She banged the empty box on a shelf and stumped out of the room, her short, stout body bumping into the doorjamb.

Angry and frustrated, Graham scuffed his way to school. Whoever had lied about him had got him in real trouble this time. Oh, he had been in scrapes before, the kind all boys get into, but he'd never been accused of stealing. And lying, too. It was probably Tony Scooter. Tony was a mean bully, always trying to get other boys in trouble.

All afternoon Graham worried. The headmaster, Mr. Prentice, who was teaching them history that day, cracked the pointer over his knuckles twice to get his attention. Rubbing his sore knuckles Graham made up his mind what he was going to do. He decided to run away from home.

Home was a ten-room house in Bury St. Edmunds that Mother Button kept for homeless boys. The house was called Velma Villa, after Mother Button whose Christian name was Velma. Velma Villa was a big, square, white stucco house criss-crossed with black wooden slats. It had four large front windows and a heavy black door that opened out onto the pavement.

There were ten boys there, half of them orphans, like Graham, and the other half war evacuees from London who hadn't returned home yet because their houses had been bombed out. The evacuees thought they were better than the orphans because they got parcels in the post and visitors on weekends. But to give Mother her due, she treated them all alike. Her daughter, Flossie, a pretty girl with flossy fair hair like spun sugar, and Auntie

Murna, a tiny lady with a hump on her back, helped Mother look after the lot of them.

Mother Button was usually very fair, but to accuse him of stealing wasn't fair at all. So at the end of the school day he hightailed it in the opposite direction instead of going home to face the music (actually a whacking with the wooden spoon on the palms of his hands — he could feel the sting just thinking about it). He had always planned to find his real mother and this seemed like a good day to start looking.

Graham knew he had been born in a place called Islington on the outskirts of London, and that his real mother had put him in the Home for Unwanteds when he was only three weeks old. He didn't know much about his mother and he often wondered why she hadn't wanted him.

Sometimes he dreamed about what it would be like to live in a real house with a real mother and father. On the way home from school he had often seen boys and girls running into their houses. Sometimes their mothers would be waiting for them at the door. Once he had seen a boy's mother suddenly spring up off her knees — she had a spade in her hand, so she must have been gardening — and fling her arms around her son. Graham had watched, his heart thumping, as they went laughing into the house together.

* * *

Now he slowed, kicking a stone along the walkway. "If I had took the bloomin' coupons I'd go home and own up to it and take my punishment. But I don't even know where they are, so how can I give them back?" he grumbled.

He gave the stone a final kick over a hedge and heard it crack on a windowpane, so he broke into a run. "If I find my real mother," he thought as he rounded a corner and slowed to a walk again, "she'll fix everything. I know she will. Why, she's probably looking for me right now all over London." After all, he reasoned, how could she know that he had been moved from the Home for Unwanteds in London to Velma Villa in Bury St. Edmunds? Maybe nobody told her. Not much wonder she hadn't been able to find him.

Once he had asked Mother Button if she knew where the Home for Unwanteds was and she had said she knew where it used to be, but it had been bombed during the Blitz and levelled to the ground. So there was no use looking for it. In fact, his mother probably thought that he was dead in the bombing, and might not be looking for him at all. She'd be so thrilled to discover he was alive!

After strolling around town for about an hour he sat down on a wooden bench near a bus stop to think about what to do next. The clock on the church tower across the street gonged five-thirty. Tea time. His stomach was rumbling like thunder and he was breaking wind by the peck. He always did that when he was empty and it had earned him the nickname of Stinker. A fat lady who was sitting beside him on the bench gave him a disgusted look and shoved over.

He could picture the tea table at home. Auntie Murna was their cook — "chief cook and bottle washer," she called herself — and she often reminded them that they were lucky to have her. It was true. The boys always looked forward to their supper. In spite of food rationing

Auntie Murna often surprised them with good things she made up right out of her head. Flossie had nicknamed these mysterious concoctions "brain pudding." Auntie Murna always said real cooks didn't need a cookbook to tell them what to do.

The baker noticed him standing there but he didn't send him away. Graham thought that was a good sign so he waited patiently. He kept his mouth clamped shut but the drool still leaked out the corners. He wiped it away with his thumb and finger.

At last the shop was empty and the baker turned the sign around on the door so it read Closed from the outside. Before he shut the door he lifted two spiky eyebrows and his spectacles went sliding down his nose. Peering at Graham over the steel rims, he asked, "Are you hungry, lad?"

The man had a nice kind voice so Graham said yes. The baker beckoned him inside and Graham watched, entranced, as he put three leftover currant buns and a steak and kidney pie into a paper bag.

"There you are then, lad. That should do until you get home. But you'd better hurry along. Your mother will be missing you."

"Thank you, sir!" called Graham over his shoulder as he hightailed it out the door.

Stopping up the street, he opened the bag, stuck his nose inside and inhaled. O, heavenly smell! Scrunching the bag shut he ran all the way to the train station at the far end of the street. A railway wagon had been shunted over onto a siding. Graham took a quick glance around. There was no one in sight so he climbed in.

The wagon was empty except for an orange crate

lying on its side and a crumpled blanket in a dusky corner. He shook the blanket out and waited for the dust to settle. Then he knelt on it so he wouldn't get splinters in his bare knees from the rough wood floor. Using the orange crate for a table, he tore open the bag and spread out his supper.

The pie was still warm from the oven. He ate it first, refusing to hurry, then he ate every last crumb of the currant buns.

Well, not quite. A few bits had scattered around him on the rumpled blanket. He heard an odd little squeak. Keeping his neck stiff, he glanced out the corner of his eye and spied a tiny grey mouse, no bigger than a man's thumb. The little creature stood perfectly still on its hind legs, its tiny front paws clasped together like hands; it stared at Graham with its bright little brown-button eyes. Graham sat stock-still, not wanting to scare the mouse away, because it was nice to have company. Between the two of them, like Jack Spratt and his wife, they "licked the platter clean."

It was quite dark now, and his full stomach made him feel drowsy. Carefully, so as not to frighten the mouse away, he gathered up the smelly blanket — in his hunger, he hadn't noticed it was smelly before — and spread it out again in the dusky corner. Then he curled up on it and whispered, "Here, Sparky, here, Sparky!" The little mouse flicked his ears as if he knew his name. Then he crept timidly onto the corner of the blanket and hunkered down not six inches from Graham's nose.

Graham wondered if he had been missed yet. He didn't think so — Mother Button had called after him as he left for school, "No supper for you tonight, Graham

6

Robbertson! I don't want to lay eyes on you again until morning." She would think he had gone home and crept up the back stairs to the bedroom.

He didn't mean to fall asleep. He meant to lie awake all night and make plans for the search for his mother. But the next thing he knew sunlight was streaming into the wagon and a tall railway man was casting a long shadow over him.

"On your feet there, laddie, or I'll have to call the police," said the man prodding him with a stick. "Loiterers are not allowed on railway property. What are you up to anyway? Haven't you got a home to go to?"

Graham scrambled to his feet and brushed the dirt off his short trousers. He gave a quick glance around for Sparky but the little mouse seemed to have disappeared.

"Well, are you going to tell me where you live?" The man's voice was gruff but not unkind. "Where's your mother?"

That question brought Graham's muddled mind back into focus. "She's over there with all them people waiting for the train," he lied, pointing to the railway platform where people were swarming around like ants on a sandhill.

"Well, off you go, then, and I hope you find her."

"I hope so, too," agreed Graham. Then he jumped out the door onto the ground. Just as he landed he caught sight of Sparky standing on his hind legs staring at him. The mouse's brown eyes sparkled like glass in the April sun.

Chapter 2

The First Search

Dashing over to the railway platform, Graham joined a group of schoolchildren waiting for the seven o'clock train to London. Mixing in among them he managed to sneak on without a ticket.

His stomach was grumbling with hunger and he couldn't hold back the wind. The boy sitting next to him wriggled his nose and cried, "Eww! There's a stinker in here!" Graham stared out the window and pretended it wasn't him.

The first thing Graham wanted to do when he got to London was find the place called Islington where he had started this life. He knew that much because it said so on his birth certificate. The certificate had been pinned to his blanket when his mother had left him at the Home for Unwanteds. Then it had followed him to Velma Villa and Mother Button had put it away in a safety box and hidden the key. But she had let him read it once and he had memorized every word.

```
Date of birth: June 2nd, 1935
Name: Neill Graham Robbertson
Mother's name: Marietta Robbertson
```

The space for a father's name had been left blank. So he didn't know if Robbertson, with two b's, was his mother's name or his father's. Or why, even though his first name was Neill, he had always been known as Graham. He wondered about that, too. Had his mother told the lady at the Home for Unwanteds to call him by his second name for some special reason? Had he been named after his father? Or his grandfather, perhaps?

Before too long he was in London, trying to figure out which bus went to Islington, and how he was going to get on it without a penny in his pocket. Then, as luck would have it, a tall man in a black business suit and bowler hat dropped his brolly and it clattered out onto the road. The man leaned over awkwardly, trying to reach it, and Graham noticed two things: the man had a stiff right leg (probably wooden because he'd lost his real one in the war, Graham thought), and a double-decker bus was coming full speed. So Graham darted onto the road, grabbed the brolly, and darted back with just inches to spare between his backside and the bus.

He handed the brolly back and the man said, "Why thank you, lad. Here's something for your trouble." And he gave Graham half a crown.

Graham knew he'd spoilt his good deed by taking money for it — Mother had taught the boys that virtue was its own reward — but this time he needed the money more than virtue. "Thank you, sir," he said, touching his cap. "Could you tell me if this here bus goes to a place called Islington?"

"It does, indeed. Hop on and I'll show you the way." The brolly man paid both their fares and Graham put the half-crown into the pocket of his short trousers. All the boys at Velma Villa wore short trousers no matter what age they were.

Graham wanted to dash up the spiral staircase to the upper deck but he thought he should sit with the man who had paid his fare. They took the seat behind the driver. Graham could feel the man sizing him up so he turned his head away and stared out the window. The bus passed a bombed-out building with no roof and a caved-in wall. His stomach rumbled ominously. As soon as he got to Islington he would buy himself a bang-up breakfast. He felt the half-crown in his pocket. He wished Mother Button would buy them long trousers. He was sure he'd look years older in long trousers.

"How old are you, son?"

Graham jumped. "I'm twelve going on thirteen." The lie popped off his tongue as easy as a spitball.

"You're very small for your age," the man remarked.

"I know," Graham agreed. "I take after my father. He's small too."

"And what's your name?"

"Neill Graham." At least that wasn't a lie.

"And where do you live?"

"In Bury St. Edmunds." That wasn't a lie either.

"Never heard of it," said the man. "It's an odd name. Is it a town or village?"

"Town. It's called Bury St. Edmunds because St. Edmund was buried there hundreds of years ago."

"I see. Very interesting. And why are you going to Islington?"

Graham felt like telling the man to mind his own business. He began to wish he'd never rescued that bloomin' brolly. But if he hadn't he wouldn't be sitting on the bus to Islington, would he?

"I'm going to visit my Auntie Murna. She promised to meet me at the bus depot." The lies slid off his tongue as smooth as butter.

"I see. Well, here's my stop." The man stood up and Graham heard his knee crack. "Islington is a few more stops, so keep a sharp lookout. And have a good time with your Auntie."

"Thank you, sir." Graham breathed a sigh of relief as he waved goodbye to his benefactor.

On the way to Islington the bus passed a whole block of bombed-out buildings. A huge crane was swinging a giant iron ball at one of the still-standing walls. Graham stretched his neck out the window as the wrecking-ball smashed into the brick wall, and the crash nearly burst his eardrums. His ears were still humming as the bus pulled into Islington Depot.

Chapter 3

Memories

The first thing he did in Islington was find a cafe and order a good English breakfast: two scrambled eggs, two rashers of bacon and bangers and fried bread and a pot of tea. He lingered over the tea thinking about his life, all eleven years of it, and what was to become of him now.

He recalled the day the Matron had told him he was to be moved from the Home for Unwanteds in London to Mother Button's foster home in Bury St. Edmunds. He had been six years old. When he had first heard the word "mother" his heart had leapt with hope. Had she come, at last, to claim him? But no, when he was delivered to Velma Villa, he found out that a foster mother was not a real mother after all.

But he liked Mother Button just the same. She was a short, stout lady with a big bosom, frizzy brown hair and wire-rimmed glasses. She was a good foster mother, strict but fair. He had soon learned that you never got paddled with the big wooden spoon unless you really deserved it. Until yesterday, that was.

Nine boys already lived there, and when Graham first arrived he had been the youngest. The boys ranged in age up to fourteen and some of the big boys were bullies. But Mother and Auntie Murna and Mother's daughter, Flossie, kept a watchful eye on the smaller boys, so it wasn't a bad home to be in if you didn't have a real home of your own.

Twice Graham had nearly been adopted. The first time he was seven years old. Mother Button had sponged and pressed his Sunday suit and kissed him goodbye at the door. He had been surprised to feel a warm tear fall from her eye right onto his cheek.

The house was in the country, and was very large. He remembered being surprised that the people who were supposed to adopt him already had a boy of their own. He was seven, too, and his name was Randolph. The lady said, "Randolph, this is Graham. He has come to be your friend." And Graham wondered why she hadn't said, "He has come to be your brother."

Another thing he remembered about that house was the big kitchen and all the black iron pots hanging on the wall. He had his meals in that kitchen, with the servants, and even at seven years old he knew this meant he was never going to be their real son, like Randolph. After a few days a man came from the children's home to see how he was settling in. The cook told him that Graham was not being treated like one of the family, so the man took him straight back to Velma Villa.

He was glad to be home again and Mother and Auntie Murna and Flossie had made a big fuss over him. But the three oldest boys gave him a pounding that first night because it meant they had to sleep three in a bed again.

14

His next chance for adoption had come when he was eight. Mr. and Mrs. Walter Witherspoon took him to their thatched cottage in Staffordshire. They had no children of their own and they seemed to like him a lot. He was happy enough there and he often wondered what might have happened if Mr. Witherspoon hadn't up and died suddenly, exactly three weeks to the day Graham had arrived. Poor Mrs. Witherspoon, she went all to pieces and she told him that she was sorry but she had to go live with her sister in Durham. And her sister was a spinster who didn't like children, so once again Graham was sent back to Velma Villa.

He never got another chance after that. Flossie said the older you got, the less people wanted you. Mother said it was a shame, but that was the way of the world. "Well, I don't care," Graham had said, "because I like it better here anyway." Mother had smiled at that and pinched his cheek.

The waitress who had brought his breakfast was standing over him dangling a wet dishrag in front of his nose. "Do you want something more?" she snapped.

"No, thank you." His answer was more polite than her question.

"Well, off you go, then." She waved him away with the dishrag. "There's people waiting for this table."

Chapter 4

Inquiries

He searched all day long in Islington. First he went to the address he had memorized from his birth certificate: number 60 Lattice Lane. It was a pretty little house with a window box full of spring flowers. There was a round bell on the door with a little butterfly-key on it. He twisted the wings and heard it bring-bring-bring inside. His heart began to pound. What if it was her, his real mother, who answered the door? Would she be surprised and happy? Or would she be surprised and mad?

A lady in a hairnet, with a feather duster in her hand, opened the door. She had a long nose and a mole on her chin with a white whisker curling out of it.

"What is it you want?" The whisker jiggled as she spoke. Graham was sure she couldn't be his mother (thank goodness!) because she looked too old. Still, removing his cap, he said, "Does Marietta Robbertson, with two b's, still live here?"

The woman frowned and pulled her head back inside. All he could see now was her nose and the jiggly

whisker. "I've never heard of a Marietta Robbertson, wi
two b's or one," she snapped and shut the door in his
face. He heard her slide the bolt. Who did she think he
was, a robber? or maybe Jack the Ripper? The thought
made him snicker out loud.

Wandering aimlessly down the street he wondered
what to do next. On the corner of Lattice Lane and
Battersby Street there was a sweetshop which reminded
him of the bloomin' sweet coupons. The lovely smell of
chocolate drew him in by his nose, like a magnet.

The man behind the counter wore a white apron over
his round stomach. Long hairs lay on his pink scalp like
brown yarn. "What's your pleasure?" he asked, pointing
to a tray of chocolate swirls.

Graham's stomach rumbled longingly. He forced his
eyes away from the sweets. "Could you tell me where the
Registry Office is?" he asked. He remembered the name
of the building from his birth certificate.

"Why do you want to know?" The man instantly acted
suspicious. Why were all grown-ups suspicious? Graham
wondered.

"My mother wants a copy of my birth certificate."
Another lie. But he couldn't help lying, could he, when
people kept asking him questions that were none of their
business?

"Well, it used to be here on Battersby Street but the
building's gone now. Bombed out. Demolished by a buzz
bomb. A direct hit, it was. I was Warden during the war
and I helped dig the people out. All killed, they were."

"I'm dreadful sorry," Graham said.

Wagging his head sadly, the man waddled out from
behind the counter and lifted the lid off a jar of jelly

babies. "Help yourself," he said and Graham reached in and scooped up a handful. "Thank you very much, sir," he said, popping two of them into his mouth.

Then the shopkeeper stepped out the door onto the pavement and pointed up the street. "It's up there, what's left of it, behind that high wire fence."

"Thanks again," Graham called over his shoulder as he ran up the street.

On the fence was a big red warning sign: DANGER, KEEP OUT! Threading his fingers through the wire mesh, Graham climbed to the top like a monkey and stared over the iron rail at the ruins of the Registry Office. Piles of rubble twenty feet high covered the whole city block.

"Cor!" he cried, jumping down. "I'll never find myself now, will I?"

On the opposite side of the street stood an old stone church. He crossed over and sat down on the worn steps. Then he popped another jelly baby into his mouth and counted what was in his pocket. Only five left. He stuffed them back into his pocket to save them for supper.

The church was surrounded by falling-down tomb-stones covered in green moss. Carved over the archway, in crumbling letters, were the words, "St. Wilfred's Anglican Church. 1621 A.D." A sign among the tomb-stones, almost hidden by weeds, read: "Reverend James Garland, Vicar." The church doors were wide open. "I might as well go in, mightn't I?" Graham told himself.

Placing his feet in the hollows of the flagstone steps, he thought of the thousands of feet that must have tread upon them to wear them so thin.

It was dark inside the church, and he had to wait until

his eyes adjusted. Then, by the light slanting through the stained-glass windows, he saw a man in a cassock kneeling at the altar. The vicar, Graham guessed. He walked softly up the aisle so as not to disturb the man, but the vaulted ceiling echoed his footsteps. He stopped suddenly when the priest stood up and turned around. "Can I help you, son?" he asked.

Graham didn't answer right away because he was staring at the christening font, imagining his mother standing there holding a baby — him — in her arms. "Maybe I was christened here," he said, half to himself.

"What makes you think so?" asked the clergyman.

"I was born in Islington."

"But you don't know if you were christened in this church?"

"No, sir, not for sure."

"Well, then, let's have a look. Come along with me."

To the right of the altar was a small door in the same arched shape as the big door. The vicar had to duck so as not to bang his head. Graham felt the tuft of hair that stood up on the crown of his head brush the top of the doorframe.

The room was very small. A massive desk and chair almost filled it. Unlocking the desk drawer with a large key, the churchman lifted out a big leather-bound book and opened it on the desk. A musty smell escaped the pages.

"Tell me what you know about yourself," the vicar said.

"Well, my name is Neill Graham Robbertson and my mother's name is Marietta Robbertson. Robbertson is spelled with two b's."

"And your father, what might his name be?"

"I don't know. It's not on my birth certificate."

"I see. Do you have the certificate with you?"

"No, sir. The lady I live with keeps it locked in a safety-box. But I got all what it says up here." He tapped his forehead.

"Well, then, do you remember the number on the top right hand corner? And your birth date?"

"Yes, sir. The number is 113528 and I was born June 2nd, 1935."

Graham's heart began to hammer as the man leafed through the book. He ran his finger down several pages and then shook his head. "I'm afraid you were never christened here, Neill." Graham's face fell and the vicar said, "I'm sorry I can't help you, lad."

"Thank you, sir." Graham had to swallow the lump which had suddenly swelled up in his throat. He didn't even explain that he was not called Neill.

By the time the sun had set he was hungry again. The jelly babies were gone and, because he was full of air instead of food, his stomach was growling. He had spent all his money on breakfast, and he had no bus fare. So he found another railway station and climbed into a wagon.

But this time he wasn't so lucky. He got caught by the station master, who called the police, who took him straight back to Bury St. Edmunds.

* * *

Mother Button was furious. "You're going straight to bed without your tea!" she snapped at him.

Graham's stomach felt like it was caving in. "I haven't et since yesterday," he said, blinking back the tears.

"Ah, now, Mum." Flossie was standing on the stairs

pulling a long face. "Have a heart. You won't do it again, will you, Graham?"

"No, never!" He shook his head vigorously. "I'm ever so sorry, Mother," he apologized. "If I promise never to run off again, may I please have some supper?"

Giving her head a shake, she grabbed him by the ear and marched him down the hall to the kitchen where the large stewpot was steaming on the big black cooker. "Turn yourself around," she ordered. He knew what was coming but he wasn't scared. Turning around he bent over with his hands on his knees. Whack! Whack! Whack! went the wooden spoon on the seat of his pants. It didn't smart half so much as a whacking on bare hands.

"There. Now sit yourself down, if you can." He was just about to say he was sorry again when she waggled the wooden spoon in his face. "I don't want to hear another word out of you tonight," she warned. So he clamped his mouth shut as she served him up a bowl of steaming beef stew and a thick crust of bread. He ate ravenously, mopped his plate with the crust of bread, and went quietly to bed.

As it turned out the sweet coupons had been taken by one of the evacuees, but no one ever apologized to Graham for falsely accusing him. Not even Mother.

Chapter 5

The Second Search

Graham managed to stay out of trouble for six whole weeks. Then one day Mother sent him to the fish and chip shop for Saturday night's supper.

Graham thought there was no other smell in all the world half so scrumptious as the lovely aroma of frying cod and chips. The smell started his mouth drooling so bad he had to wipe it with his hanky as he waited. Mother always made the boys carry a hanky. She wanted them to grow up to be gentlemen, she said, and gentlemen always carried hankies.

The man in the greasy apron wrapped two big piles of fish and chips in double newspapers and stacked them in Graham's arms. The packets were so high they touched his chin and the delicious smell seeped through the newspapers, right up his nose.

As he hurried home the parcels shifted and he was afraid the top one was going to slide right off. So he stopped and lowered them onto a low stone wall. The hot grease had leaked through the paper and the lovely smell had leaked out with it. His mouth filled with water, and his fingers trembled greedily as he began picking a hole through the spreading dark patch.

He only meant to eat one chip, or maybe two. But by the time he got back to the Villa the top packet was half empty. Mother was furious. "Graham," she cried, her dark eyes flashing, "you are a wicked, wicked boy and I must punish you."

"I know." He shrugged his shoulders and held out both hands. Squeezing his eyes shut, he winced as the wooden spoon landed, Smack! Smack! Smack! three times on each palm.

"Now off to bed with you," she said, and smacked the seat of his pants for good measure.

He knew he deserved the punishment, but his smarting hands and the laughter coming from the kitchen as the other boys enjoyed what was left of the fish and chips filled him with fury instead of remorse. He hadn't had one piece of fish!

So what should he do? He could either go downstairs and beg forgiveness or he could run off again.

He went to bed with his clothes on under his nightshirt. Then he began reminiscing about the other time he'd run away. "That was a lovely pie the bakeshop man gave me," he thought, licking his lips. "And what a smart little friend Sparky was." He smiled as he pictured the tiny mouse who had shared his supper. "And most of the people I met were nice: the brolly man and the sweet shop man and the vicar." Hugging his knees to his chest he grinned in the dark. "It was lots of fun," he thought, forgetting all about the trouble he'd got himself into.

When the other boys came up to bed he pretended to

be asleep by snoring softly. Little Ernie Moore crept into bed beside him. Graham was glad he shared the bed with a smaller boy who was timid, like Sparky the mouse, and was afraid to even wiggle his toes in bed. The boys called him Twiddle because that's what he did with his hair, twiddled it round and round his finger. All the boys at Velma Villa had nicknames: Tony was Picker because his finger was always halfway up his nose; Tom was Pieface because he'd got caught nicking Auntie Murna's black-berry pie off the windowsill; Benny was Bulldog because he looked like one, and Graham was Stinker, of course.

Graham was still wide awake when dawn began creep-ing in the window. "It's now or never," he thought. Easing himself out of bed so as not to waken Twiddle, he picked up his boots and crept down the stairs, carefully avoiding the creaky board. As he passed through the pantry he spied a bag of buns on the sideboard. He snatched it up, then slipped out the kitchen door. On the back step he pulled on his boots and made a dash for the railway sta-tion.

He caught the early train and headed straight back to London. Again he didn't have any money, but he man-aged to avoid the ticket collector on the train by hiding in the lavatory. It was a damp, chilly May morning and the fog hadn't lifted yet. But by the time he got to Picadilly Circus a warm spring breeze had blown the mist away.

Leaning on the iron fence that enclosed the Circus, he watched as dozens of black taxi cabs darted like water beetles around the statue of Eros. The first time he saw Picadilly Circus, he had been disappointed because there were no lions or tigers or elephants there. Flossie had laughed and said, "It's not that kind of circus, Graham."

24

Then she had explained that the statue of Eros was the god of love. He thought Eros was a poor substitute for tigers jumping through fiery hoops.

Graham managed to escape the ticket collector on the tube by dashing with the crowd from car to car at each station. He got all the way to Admiralty Arch without spending a penny.

Looking up the long pink mall, he could see Queen Victoria's statue sitting on its high stone pedestal in front of Buckingham Palace. So he decided to visit the King and Queen . . .

He had been to Buckingham Palace once before, the day that Mother had brought the boys to London's Childrens' Hospital for X-rays to make sure they didn't have TB. Afterwards, for a treat, she had marched them single file up the Mall. The boys hated "walking crocodile" because it made them look like Home boys, which they were, but they didn't want every Tom, Dick and Harry in London to know it.

Well, as luck would have it, there had been no flag flying on top of the Palace that day, and Flossie had explained that no flag meant King George and Queen Elizabeth and the little princesses were not at home, so they had all gone back to Bury St. Edmunds disappointed. But today Graham saw the Royal Standard snapping in the breeze. He raced up to the black iron gates that were tipped with gold and stared at the wonder of the Palace. He must have stood there for two hours, making faces at the palace guards in their scarlet coats and black fur busbies, but Princess Elizabeth and Princess Margaret Rose never showed their royal noses at the windows. "Blow!" he said. "I'm never going to see them, am I?"

Disappointed, he wandered off again and ended up in Hyde Park.

He had heard about Speaker's Corner in Hyde Park where people stood on soapboxes and said nasty things about the Royals and the Prime Minister and the government and they never got arrested because you could say what you liked at Speaker's Corner. But on this particular day he was surprised to see the park was cordoned off by a yellow police line and bobbies were ordering crowds of people to "Stand back, if you please."

Graham pushed his way to the front of the crowd and wedged in between a fat man and a lady holding a baby. "What's going on?" he asked her.

"They've found an unexploded bomb in the park." The lady pointed to where a group of army men were busy doing something. "They're the bomb squad," she explained.

"They're trying to defuse a buzz bomb," the fat man said.

"Cor!" exclaimed Graham.

A short time later a soldier in army fatigues stood on one of the speaker's boxes and shouted through a megaphone. "It's all over, folks. The bomb's been defused so you can be on your way."

There was a rousing cheer for the bomb squad. Then the police took the yellow line down and the excitement was over.

"Goodbye, then." The lady swung the baby, dressed in a sailor suit, onto her other hip. Suddenly, she seemed familiar to Graham. "Goodbye, Missus . . . Missus . . . does your name happen to be Robbertson?" he asked.

"No," she gave a little laugh. "It's Pomeroy. Rachel

Pomeroy. Why do you ask?"

"Oh," he shrugged. "It ain't important."

"Well, ta-ta, then," she said. "Be good."

Graham heard Big Ben striking in the distance, so he counted the gongs. "Twelve," he said. "Lunchtime. I wonder what Auntie Murna made for dessert today? Maybe a jam roly-poly with custard sauce." The thought made his mouth all drooly. So he stopped on a green wooden bench and ate his bread buns. He wished he'd had time to butter them. He shook out the crumbs for the pigeons and got a drink at the water fountain.

A big woman walked down the gravel path tugging a little boy by the hand. The boy stuck out his tongue at Graham. So Graham stuck his out in return and they both laughed.

The woman made Graham think of his mother. Except she was too big. In his mind's eye he pictured his mother short and stocky, like himself, with brown hair and hazel eyes. Just then another woman went hurrying by carrying two Marks and Spencer shopping bags. She matched the picture of his mother to a T so he ran up to her and said, "Excuse me, but is your name Marietta Robbertson with two b's?"

"Certainly not," she snapped and kept on walking. "How dare you accost me. Go away or I'll call the police."

The next lady who fit the picture went strolling by pushing a pram. She was leaning forward, chattering baby talk to a chubby infant in a pink bonnet and matching coat.

"If that lady was my mother," Graham thought, tingling with excitement, "then the baby would be my sister, wouldn't she?"

He caught up to her and fell into step. "Your baby is pretty," he said to the lady. "What's her name?"

"Daphne," she said. "What's yours?"

"Graham," he said. "Graham Robbertson. Might that be your name too? Robbertson with two b's."

"That's an odd question." She looked at him curiously. "Why do you ask?"

"Because you look like a picture of my mother. I was hoping you might be her. I haven't seen her for a long time you see." He didn't tell her the picture was a figment of his imagination.

"Well, I'm sorry to say my name is Mrs. Flaherty, but I wouldn't mind a bit having a boy like you." She gave him a warm smile. "Where do you live, then, if not with your mother?"

"Oh, I live with a very kind lady," he assured her.

"Well, I'm glad to hear that," she said. "And there's my own mother waiting for me now." An older woman wearing a headscarf was waving from the corner. Mrs. Flaherty waved back. "Goodbye, Graham. Good luck!" The wheels of the pram went clickety-click and the baby clapped her hands as they hurried off.

During the day he must have asked twenty-five ladies, and most of them snapped at him, "No!" or "Be on your way." Only the lady with the baby had been nice, as he was sure his own mother would have been.

By the time the sun set the air had turned damp and cold. He wished he'd brought his woollen pullover. Mother and Flossie had knitted all the boys thick navy-blue pullovers for Christmas. Auntie Murna couldn't knit anymore because her fingers were too gnarled with rheumatism.

Tired and discouraged, he found the nearest railway siding and curled up in the corner of an empty wagon. There was no warm pie and no blanket and no mouse this time. But he was so tired he fell asleep almost instantly on the bare board floor.

The next morning he walked up and down narrow side streets, hungry and miserable, looking for breadshops. "I'll ask have they got any stales," he thought. "And I'll offer to sweep the floor to pay for them." He found a cakeshop but it was closed and then he heard church bells, reminding him it was Sunday. Around the side of the shop he could see a yellow seedcake in the window. His stomach knotted at the sight. He glanced over his shoulder in both directions; the street was empty. Suddenly hunger got the better of him and he smashed his fist through the window. The glass exploded with an ear-splitting crash that scared the wits out of him. He grabbed the cake and fled.

He ran like the wind, his heart thumping. What if somebody had heard the crash? At last he stopped, gasping for air, and collapsed on a wooden bench. Then he looked at the cake in his hand. There were droplets of blood mixed with the seeds on top. He turned his wrist over and saw a jagged line of clotted blood. He'd cut himself and hadn't even felt it. Speckles of glass glittered like sugar on top the cake. He picked out the glass and bits of blood. Then he gobbled up every crumb, and nothing ever tasted so good.

Feeling much better now that his stomach was full he began to get nervy. "Mother must have the police looking for me by now," he thought, "so if I walk real cockylike maybe they won't suspect I'm a runaway." He was strutting along the platform at Charing Cross Station when a policeman nabbed him by the shoulder. "What's your name, boy, and where do you live? And don't lie or it'll be Borstal for you."

Borstal! The name of the infamous remand home for bad boys knocked the cockiness right out of him. "My name's Graham Robbertson and I live in Bury St. Edmunds," he answered meekly.

Grabbing him by the scruff of the neck, the copper marched Graham into the station master's office and plunked him down on a chair. Then he picked up the telephone and dialled. "I think I've found the lost boy from Bury St. Edmunds," he said, keeping his eyes glued on Graham. "Aye, he fits that description."

"Cor blimey, what'll I do now?" worried Graham. Then the answer popped into his head like a flashbulb.

"Please, sir, may I go to the toilet?" he asked, crossing his legs because he really did have to go. The policeman pointed to the door marked GENTS LAVATORY and Graham dashed in. After going he washed his hands from habit — Mother had a terrible fear of germs.

His plan was to climb out a window but he spied a door opposite to the one he'd just come in. He had to think fast. He glanced at the wooden cistern up near the ceiling above the toilet. A chain with a knob on the end hung down from it. Grabbing the knob. he gave it a hard yank. The sudden downpour of flushing water covered the scraping noise as he pulled open the door. Poking his head out he saw that it led to a back lane. The lane was empty so he took off like a shot.

The minute he was free his cockiness returned. He chuckled to himself at the thought of the dressing-down that poor bobby would get when he had to admit that the lost boy he had just found was lost again.

Graham spent the whole afternoon walking about London feeling free as the pigeons that swooped through the air. Strolling along the Embankment, by the River Thames, he gazed up at Cleopatra's Needle. "When I grow up I think I'll live in London," he decided. "There's bound to be lots of jobs of work in such a busy place."

But all the time he was sightseeing, he never lost track of his quest to find his mother. He looked at every woman who even came close to matching the picture he carried in his mind. If she looked back at him he smiled winningly and asked her name. But none of them were Robbertsons.

Wandering around from place to place, he found himself on a bridge spanning the river. From there he could see the Tower of London. He remembered hearing the story of the little princes who had been murdered there. "Cor," he thought with a shiver. "Wouldn't I like to see that place!"

He was trying to think of a way to get there when it began to rain, a misty rain, at first, then it came down in buckets. Hundreds of brollies sprang up like blackbirds' wings and people ran for cover. The only shelter he could find was a bench in a nearby park. London was full of benches. He rolled underneath it and curled up in a ball to wait it out.

That was his big mistake. He hadn't realized how tired he was until he was startled awake by a sharp jab in the ribs.

"Come out from there, you young vagrant." A giant

copper was leaning down, prodding him with his truncheon.

Soaking wet and shivering, Graham crawled out from under the bench and got to his feet.

"What's your name and where do you come from?" The copper wagged the truncheon in Graham's face. Graham knew, then, that the game was up. He told the copper what he wanted to know. Tears welled up in Graham's eyes and he couldn't stop them spilling down his face. Once again he was brought back to Velma Villa in disgrace.

"He is to be kept under house arrest until further notice," the policeman told Mother Button. "Do you understand me, madam?"

"Indeed I do." Mother Button bristled and shoved Graham behind her broad backside. "You're not talking to an ignoramus you know. I'm a businesswoman. Who do you think pays your wages?"

The policeman became suddenly respectful. "I beg your pardon, madam. But this youngster here needs to be dealt with."

"You leave him to me. I know how to deal with boys. Now off you go and catch some thief that's busy robbing innocent folk blind while you're wasting your time and mine."

Slamming the door she marched Graham down the hall ahead of her, her finger poking between his shoulder blades.

"Cor, Mother! You sure told him!" Graham snickered.

"You be quiet." She boxed both his ears. "You'll abide by my rules or you'll rue the day. Now get upstairs and wash that grin off your face."

Chapter 6

The Escort

"I've never been so disappointed," Mother Button grumbled as she bustled about the kitchen. "I thought you were a good boy, I really did."

"She really did," Flossie agreed, shaking her flossy blond head. "Mother always says, 'Graham is a good boy.'"

"Aye," agreed Auntie Murna looking up from the pie crust she was pinching. "I heard her say so with my own ears."

Mother Button gave an exasperated sigh. "You have a good home here, Graham. I've been told by lots of folks that I run a good foster home. So why do you run off like that?"

Graham was determined not to tell anybody about his search for his real mother. Especially Mother Button, for fear of hurting her feelings. So he shrugged his shoulders and said, "I don't know."

For the rest of the school term Mother Button decreed that Graham had to be escorted back and forth to school. It was the only place he was allowed to go while under house arrest. The boy she had chosen for his escort (more like a jailer, Graham thought) was none other than Tony Scooter, the nose-picker.

"Why are you walking with Stinker?" the other boys scoffed at Tony.

"Because he's under house arrest and I'm the law," bragged Tony, his little finger poking at his nose.

"Hey, is that right, Stink? Did the coppers really collar you?" asked Benny-the-bulldog.

"Sure they did." Graham began to swagger. "But I gave them the slip lots of times before they caught me."

"Tell us where you went and what you done!" Pieface Riddle stood in front of Graham with his feet apart and his arms crossed over his thick chest. He was Tony's best mate, and a bully, too.

It was the first time the big boys had ever bothered with Graham except to give him a quick punch when nobody was looking. So he promptly made up a story about visiting Buckingham Palace and waving to the little princesses at the palace window. "You should see them," he bragged. "They're even prettier than their pictures."

By the time they got to school he had told a string of stories, none of which were true. He had no intention of telling anybody about his search for his mother.

Miss Featherstone had been their teacher since the beginning of term. She didn't seem to like Graham very much.

"I heard Mr. Prentice tell Miss Featherstone that you were a troublemaker," Colleen McIntyre had confided.

There were only ten girls in the whole school and

Colleen was the prettiest. She had long red curls and freckles on her nose and green eyes with sweeping red lashes. All the boys had a crush on Colleen.

To catch Colleen's attention, while Miss Featherstone had her back turned writing on the chalk-board, he began flicking spitballs of blotting paper in Colleen's direction. One damp blob landed on her desk. She turned around, her red curls bouncing, and threw it back with a cheeky wink.

"Cor blimey, I think she likes me!" marvelled Graham. So he quickly chewed another chunk of blotter and launched it off his ruler. In the nick of time Colleen ducked her head and the wet blob zinged right past her and landed in the teacher's hair.

Whirling around, she picked the sticky thing out of her hair and held it at arm's length on the flat of her hand, as if it were a toad. "Who did this?" she demanded.

"Robinson did it," piped up Silas Snutch. Silas's nick-name was Snutch the Snitch.

Miss Featherstone marched over and gave Silas a soft cuff on the ear. "His name is Robbertson, not Robinson," she corrected. Then she cuffed his other ear. "And that's for telling tales."

Graham was so surprised that Miss Featherstone had taken his part that he confessed that the spitball was his.

"Then go and stand in the corner," ordered Miss Featherstone. And there he stood, for the rest of the afternoon.

* * *

On the last day of school Miss Featherstone asked the class to write an essay on what they planned to do on their summer holiday.

Graham stared at the long piece of foolscap for twenty minutes and didn't even write his name. Then Miss Featherstone collected the papers.

Leafing through them with a rubber finger cap, she stopped short and held up the empty foolscap. "Whose paper is this?" she asked.

Graham hesitated, then raised his hand.

"Why is it blank?" she questioned.

"Because . . . I don't want to tell you," he muttered.

"What did you say?"

"I said I don't want to tell you what I'm going to do on my summer holiday."

"Why not?" she demanded.

"Because it's . . . it's . . ."

"It's what?"

"It's none of your business," he blurted out.

The whole class gasped. Colleen turned around and stared at him, her bright green eyes as big as saucers.

Little red patches appeared on the teacher's high cheekbones. She smoothed her shiny black hair with her long white fingers. "Go back in your corner," she pointed.

An hour later, when the class was dismissed, Miss Featherstone said, "Come here, Graham, and stand beside my desk."

He stumbled over, his knees buckling from standing still so long.

Opening the top drawer of her desk, she took out a black leather strap and placed it on the edge of the desk.

"Graham. Do you think you deserve this?"

Keeping his head down, he muttered, "No, Miss."

"Look at me and repeat that."

He raised his eyes slowly. "No, Miss," he repeated.

"Why don't you think you deserve it?"

"Because I told the truth."

Miss Featherstone tapped her pencil in a tattoo on her desk. Graham stared down at his new summer shoes, his birthday present from Mother Button. The laces were tied in knots. "I need new shoelaces," he thought.

"Graham." The teacher's voice was gentler now.

He raised his eyes without raising his head. "Yes."

"Yes, Miss Featherstone."

"Yes, Miss Featherstone."

"What are you planning to do that you're ashamed of?"

"I ain't ashamed of nothing." His chin shot up defiantly. "I just don't want to talk about it, is all."

"But . . . if you're in some kind of trouble, perhaps I can help." She leaned forward and looked him right in the eyes. "Don't you trust me, Graham?"

Her eyes were the clearest blue he'd ever seen. "Yes, Miss Featherstone," he said.

"Well, then . . ."

"Well . . . you have to promise never to tell nobody."

"I promise never to tell anybody," she said, and crossed her heart solemnly.

He took a deep breath and let it out. "I'm going to spend the summer looking for my mother," he confessed. "Us boys at the foster home call Mother Button, Mother, but she's not our real mother."

"Is she unkind to you, Graham?"

"Oh, no, Mother's fair to all us boys. She only whacks us when we deserve it. But that doesn't make her real, does it?"

"No-o—" She put the strap and papers in the drawer and took out her purse. Then she touched him lightly on the shoulder and they walked out of the school together. Tony Scooter was swinging on the iron gate, picking his nose, waiting for him. Stopping on the top step, Graham whispered to the teacher, "I don't want him to know. I don't want nobody to know."

Smoothing down the tuft of hair that stuck up on the crown of his head, she whispered back, "You can trust me Graham. I'll never tell. But try not to get into trouble during the summer holidays. Will you promise me that, Graham?"

"Okay, Miss Featherstone, I promise. Am I dismissed?"

"Yes." She gave him a little push. "Away you go."

He jumped down the stairs and fell into step with Tony.

"What did she do to you?" questioned Tony. "What did she say? Are you in a heap of trouble? Is she going to tell Mother on you?"

With Miss Featherstone on his side, Graham wasn't afraid of anybody. "Shut up, Picker!" he yelled. Then he sprinted ahead so fast that Tony couldn't catch him.

Chapter 7

The New Boy

Graham dreaded the holidays. His house arrest was over and Tony Scooter and Tom Riddle and Benny-the-bulldog had got themselves summer jobs in town. So he was free to come and go as he liked. But he didn't know what to do with himself.

He wished he had a job, too. He had asked Mr. Widdicombe, the greengrocer, if he could be his summer help. He loved the smell of fresh fruits and vegetables. But Mr. Widdicombe had said he was too young. Maybe next year, he said. So the summer yawned ahead of him, long and boring.

Then the new boy arrived. His name was Matthew Penny.

"Matthew comes to us from Ipswich," Mother Button said, "and he's just your age, Graham, so I expect you'll be good friends." She sat the new boy next to him at the supper table.

"You two could be brothers," Flossie remarked from across the table. "There's a strong resemblance, except that Matthew's face is thinner."

They looked at each other sideways and sure enough it was true: they had the same hazelnut-coloured eyes and ears that didn't stick out and the same tuft of hair on the crown of their heads. Mother Button called it a rooster tuft. "It's a bit like looking in a mirror," Graham thought, "except he's skinnier than me."

And then he had another thought. What if . . . just what if . . . Matthew Penny turned out to be his brother? Or even his cousin? That would take the biscuit, now, wouldn't it?

Mother Button circled the table, dishing up the steaming shepherd's pie and boiled cabbage onto their plates. "Now, I want all you boys to say hello to Matthew and make him feel welcome," she said, her dark eyes sweeping around the table. So Tom and Tony said, "Hi, Skinny!" and the other boys mimicked, "Hi Skinny!" Instantly, Matthew got his nickname.

"Shush!" Mother Button wagged her finger. "No carry-on at the table. Graham, you and Matthew will be sharing the double bed."

"Oh, blow it!" Graham thought.

Ernie Moore had been adopted and Graham had had the luxury of the double bed all to himself for two whole weeks.

Now Mother Button filled each boy's mug with steaming green water from the saucepan. But she only gave Matthew half a mug.

"What's this stuff?" Matthew asked Graham in a whisper.

"It's cabbage water." Graham scooped up a spoonful and cooled it with a blow.

40

"Cabbage water! I never drank cabbage water before."

"Humph!" grunted Mother Button topping up his mug. "It's full of good vit-a-mins so drink it up," she said. "That's why my boys hardly ever get sick. I give them their vegetable juice and it keeps them healthy."

"Waste not, want not," put in Auntie Murna from her chair by the cooker. Auntie Murna always ate by herself later on.

Matthew squinted his eyes and screwed up his nose and took a sip of the steaming green water. Then he spit it back into the mug. "Eww, I don't like it," he whispered to Graham.

"Well, you can't leave the table until you drink it so hold your nose and scoff it," Graham advised. Then he drained his own mug. "You'll get used to it. And Mother's right. Us boys hardly ever get sick."

After supper the older boys were allowed to go into town to see George Formby's new film at the picture house. The younger boys went out to play marbles in the gutter. Graham and Matthew were at sixes and sevens.

"Do you like chess?" Matthew asked Graham all of a sudden.

"I don't know, I never tried it," Graham said.

"If you want I'll teach you."

Mother Button looked up from her tatting. "I'm sorry to say we don't have a chess set, but we've got a draught board. Graham is wizard at draughts."

"Then he'll catch on to chess in no time," Matthew said. "I brought my own chess set. It belonged to my father, and my grandfather before him."

"He's got a father," thought Graham. "Ain't he

lucky?" Then he said out loud, "Where's your father now, then?"

"He got himself killed," Matthew said in a flat voice.

"Blimey," Graham said. "What about your grandfather, is he dead, too?"

"Oh, yes, long ago."

The next question was hard for Graham to ask. "What about your mother?"

Matthew scowled. "You ask too many questions," he snapped and walked away.

Graham was right on his heels. "Can I see your chess set?" he asked.

"I guess so," agreed Matthew.

Graham followed his new friend . . . or at least his new bedmate . . . upstairs and Matthew lifted the honeycomb spread by the fringe and pulled out his case from under their bed. Inside on top of his things was a folded board. He opened it on the bed and dumped out a box of ivory pieces. The box and the board smelled old and musty.

"These are the men." Matthew picked up one of the pieces. "The white ones go on one side of the board and the black ones on the other. You can have the white ones."

Two hours went by like magic. They didn't even glance up when Flossie passed the open door to put the younger boys to bed. When they heard the older boys laughing and clumping up the stairs, Matthew quickly gathered up the chessmen.

"Whatcha got there?" demanded Tony Scooter coming in the door. "Give us a look."

Graham jumped up and placed himself, feet apart, hands on hips, between Matthew and Tony. "It's his

42

father's chess set and Mother Button knows all about it," he said keeping his voice steady.

Tony picked his nose thoughtfully. Even the biggest boys were a bit afraid of Mother Button. Short as she was, she could be quite fierce if she got her temper up. So he shrugged and walked away.

"Thanks mate," said Matthew shoving the case back under the bed with his foot.

"You're welcome, mate," Graham grinned, pleased with himself that he had stood up to Tony. Then he and Matthew shook hands like grown men and that was the beginning of their friendship.

Chapter 8

Pocket Money

One hot summer morning there was a loud banging on the front door of Velma Villa.

Mother Button set the iron on its stand and glanced down the hall. "Why, it's that beastly Mr. Beetle from next door," she said. He could be seen peering through the lace curtain on the door-window. "Go and see what he wants, Graham."

Graham got up from the table, where he and Matthew were playing chess again, and ran down the hall and swung open the door. Mr. Beetle hollered over Graham's head, "Mrs. Button, I want a word with you."

Mother Button took her time coming down the hall. "What is it now, Mr. Beetle?" She had to look up at him because he was at least six feet tall and Mother Button was only five feet with her shoes on. But she seemed bigger because she was a sturdy little woman with a big bottom.

"Four of your boys . . . I counted them, four . . . have been scrumping my apples. Now just because a few branches hang over into your back garden doesn't mean they are yours for the taking."

"Well, the law says . . ." Mother Button's dark little eyes began shooting sparks. "The law says that what's on my side of the line is mine," she declared. "So close the door, Graham, before Auntie Murna gets a draft." Then she turned on her heel and marched back to the kitchen. Graham laughed and shut the door in Mr. Beetle's face.

"Is that really the law, Gray?" Matthew and Graham were watching through the window curtain as Mr. Beetle stalked away.

"It is if Mother says so," Graham said.

Mother Button had resumed her ironing. "Now, then, how would you two boys like a job of work to keep you busy?" she said. "You spend far too much time over that chess board. Not that there's anything wrong with it, mind. But it keeps you indoors too much."

"What sort of job?" asked Graham.

"Well, I've decided it's about time to plant a hedgerow between us and that old billy goat next door. He's altogether too fond of gawping over here, watching every move we make."

The boys crowed at the nickname.

"If Tony and Tom were here I'd ask them because they're bigger and stronger than you boys," continued Mother Button, fitting a shirt over the narrow end of the ironing-board. "But they'll be busy working in town for the rest of the summer. So what do you say?"

"What do you want us to do?" asked Graham. "We can do anything they can, can't we, Matty?"

"Sure." Matthew crooked his skinny arm and up popped a muscle the size of a grape.

"I want a ditch dug about a foot deep from the back of the house to the fence," Mother Button said. "And I'll give you a tanner a day to share if you do a good job."

"How about a bob?" bargained Graham. A tanner was only sixpence and a bob was twice as much — a whole shilling.

"A bob! You must think money grows on trees like apples. And the way you boys eat me out of house and home I wish it did. Oh, all right then, a shilling it is if you do good work. You'll find the tools in the shelter."

The Anderson air raid shelter, shaped like an arch and made of corrugated iron, had been in the back garden since the war.

It was used for a storage shed now. Graham unlatched the door and scraped it open, and the two boys stepped inside. Gas masks still hung like skeletons from pegs along the wall.

"Which one is yours?" Matty's voice had dropped to a whisper.

"The one at the end. Let's get out of here."

Grabbing the tools, they jumped outside and banged the door shut behind them. They set to work.

"I'm not very good at this," gasped Matthew, his thin chest heaving as he struggled to break ground with the long-handled spade.

"Here, let me show you." Forcing the spade into the ground, Graham jumped on it with both feet. His weight sunk it deep into the soil and he lifted out a heap of black dirt.

Matthew's eyes shone with hero worship. "Cor, Gray, I wish I was as strong as you," he said.

Graham clenched his fist and crooked his arm and a

hard lump, shaped like a pear, swelled up on his fore-arm. He laughed, proud as punch of himself.

Halfway through the morning Graham could see that Matthew was tiring, so he said, "Time out for a drink of water." There was a water tap near the back door with a tin cup hanging on a nail beside it. Graham filled the cup and they sat on the step to share it.

"Do you like it here in Bury St. Edmunds?" asked Matthew.

"It's okay." Graham swirled water around the bottom of the cup and dripped it over his head. "But I like London better because it's bigger."

"Ipswich is bigger, too," said Matthew. "Bury's a queer little place. I wonder how it got its name?"

"Oh, I can tell you that," Graham said. "St. Edmund, you see, was king of England a long time ago and he got killed in the battle of Suffolk by the Vikings. They tied him to a tree and shot him full of arrows and when his men found him his head was gone."

"Where'd it go?" Matthew's eyes nearly popped out.

"Well, one story says it was being et by a wolf when St. Edmund's men found it. So they had to tear it out of the wolf's fangs. Then they put his body and head back together again in a sackcloth and buried him here."

"Where?"

"Nobody knows for sure. Maybe near the abbey ruins, or in the cathedral grounds. Anyway, he's buried here somewheres. That's why this town is named Bury St. Edmunds."

Matthew shuddered and changed the subject. "Who do you like best here at Velma Villa, Mother or Auntie Murna or Flossie?"

Graham frowned thoughtfully. "I like Auntie Murna's cooking best," he said. "And Flossie's a good one. Mother's all right, too, but I'm always getting into scrapes with her."

"What kind of scrapes?"

"Oh, like the time she sent me down the cellar to put shillings in the gas meter."

"Did you nick a shilling?"

"NO! I just took a swig of Mother's homemade cider is all. There were rows of bottles lined up on a shelf. It was a lovely amber colour and it looked so good I popped the cork out of a bottle and took a big swig. Then I put the cork back in and set the bottle in the back row so Mother wouldn't notice."

"Was it good?"

"Coo, was it!" Graham smacked his lips. "But what I didn't know was that it makes your breath smell funny. The minute I came up the stairs and walked past Mother's chair she grabbed me by the scruff and made me open my mouth and huff in her face."

"Then what happened?"

"I got six whacks with the wooden spoon and sent to bed with no supper." He laughed. "It's a wonder I'm not skinnier than you, Matty, I've missed so many suppers."

Flossie came outside in her yellow sundress, with a watering can. She filled the can at the tap and sprinkled the roses on the trellis by the door.

"You'd better get back to work or you'll miss another one," she teased Graham.

"See what I mean, Matt?" Graham grinned at Flossie knowing she never carried tales to her mother.

By noon they had worked their way back to the overhanging branches of Mr. Beetle's apple tree. Leaning on the spade handle, sweat running past his ears and dripping off his chin, Graham said, "It must be dinner time by now." The smell of the ripe red fruit hanging right in front of their noses made his mouth water.

Luckily, Mother came to the back door and saved them from temptation. "Come you boys, wash up for lunch," she cried.

Throwing the tools down, they dashed for the house.

"Fetch them up here by the door," she called. "I don't trust that old billy goat as far as I can throw a cow." She spoke in a loud voice and Mr. Beetle bellowed, "MOOO!" from his back porch.

Laughing, the boys retrieved the spades, leaned the long handles by the door, kicked their muddy boots off, and went inside.

They joined the noisy line of boys washing up at the scullery sink. Glancing in the cracked mirror over the sink Graham saw that his round cheeks were as red as Mr. Beetle's apples. But when Matthew washed the mud off his face, his thin cheeks were a pale yellow, like the carbolic soap they'd just washed with.

Mother noticed it and felt his forehead. Then she pinched one of his eyelids up. "Roll your eyes," she said.

Matthew's eyes, as he rolled them around, looked like bloodshot marbles.

"You go to bed and I'll have Flossie bring you up your soup," Mother said, and Graham detected worry in her voice.

"But I've got to help Graham finish the trench," protested Matthew.

"Why don't Tom and me take over the job?" suggested Tony Scooter. He and Tom had come home for lunch. Seeing the greedy glint in Tony's eyes, Graham thought, "I'll bet he's heard about the bob." Then Flossie spoke up. "No, I'll help Graham. And don't you worry, Matthew, you'll get your money."

It was fun working with Flossie. She made it more like a game than work. By the time the week was out the trench was dug and the hedge was planted. And Mother Button was as good as her word. She gave Graham and Matthew a shilling each.

Matthew spent the week in bed and then he was up and about again.

Graham's palm itched with the feel of money in his hand. "Have you got any more jobs of work?" he asked Mother Button.

"There's always plenty to do around here," she said, leaning on the broom handle. "You boys can weed and hoe the vegetable patch if Matthew feels up to it."

"I'm fine." Matthew said, flexing his puny muscles. "Fit as a fiddle, I am."

"I'll hoe," Graham volunteered, knowing that hoeing was the hardest part of the job. "And Matty can pull the weeds."

Nearly every day Mother Button found something for them to do. And if she didn't, she'd send them across the road to the Widow Tweedy's. Mrs. Tweedy lived alone and she often had little jobs that needed doing.

They both saved their money and within a couple of weeks they had a nice little bagful of coins. Dumping it out on the bed between them, they counted fourteen shillings and sixpence.

"What are you going to do with yours?" asked Matthew.

Graham had been lying awake at night thinking about that very thing. "If I tell you," he said, "you got to swear to secrecy."

"I swear." Matthew spat on his hand and stuck it out. Graham did the same and grabbed Matthew's hand. Squeezing the spit between their palms, they shook and sealed their secret.

Graham lowered his voice. "I'm going to London to have a look round for my mother," he said.

"Is she in London?"

"I think so. I've been there twice already looking for her but no luck yet. But I figure if I keep looking I'm bound to find her someday."

"Well, I've decided to go to Ipswich to visit my auntie and my cousin," said Matthew wistfully. It was the first time he'd mentioned he had relatives. Graham was dying to ask about them. But he decided to wait until Matthew was ready to tell him. "I miss my auntie a bit," continued Matthew. "And maybe she's changed her mind about me." Graham wondered what Matthew meant by that, but he held his tongue. "And, hey, maybe your mother's in Ipswich. Maybe you've been looking in the wrong city."

"Blimey, I never thought of that," said Graham.

"Would Mother Button let us go?" asked Matthew.

"No. But you could say we got invited."

"Well . . . how would I hear from them?"

The wheels had started turning in Graham's head. "Write yourself a letter," he said. "Mother don't know what your writing looks like, does she?"

"No."

"Good." Graham got paper and pencil out of his

bookbag and handed them to Matthew.

Matthew licked the lead tip. "What'll I say?" he asked.

"Write . . . Dear Matthew, we miss you. How would you like to visit us this here Sunday? We are having a family party and thought you'd want to come. You can bring a friend if you like. Sincerely, your cousin Maude."

"I don't have a Cousin Maude."

"Well, for Pete's sake, what cousin have you got then?"

"I got an aunt and uncle and a cousin Rodney."

"It's better if the invite comes from a lady. What's your aunt's name?"

"Mary. Auntie Mary."

"That's it then."

Matthew's handwriting was very fine, like a lady's. Graham had him make three copies and he chose the best one. "Now the envelope," he said. "It's got to have a stamp on it that looks like it's been franked."

"How can we do that?" Matthew looked skeptical.

"Leave it to me," Graham said. "There's always envelopes in the hall table drawer. You go sidetrack Mother while I pinch one. I better make it two in case you mess up."

Mother Button was down on her hands and knees scrubbing the kitchen lino. Strands of damp hair had escaped her hairpins and was clinging to her flushed cheeks. She glanced up when Matthew appeared in the doorway.

"Well, what is it you want?" she snapped. Scrubbing always made her short-tempered.

"I'm hungry. Can Graham and me have a bite before supper?"

"You set foot on my lino before it's dry and I'll give you more than a bite. I'll give you a good hiding. Now away with you." She shook the scrub brush at him, spraying soap suds on his shoes.

But Matthew stood his ground, distracting Mother by asking nuisance questions, until he saw Graham scoot back up the stairs.

Back in the bedroom they propped a chair against the doorknob. Graham had managed to get two new envelopes and one old one with a used stamp in the corner. Matthew addressed the two new envelopes to himself and Graham picked the best one.

"Now the stamp." Swivelling his jaws like a cow chewing its cud, Graham rolled saliva around in his mouth until he'd gathered up a good gobful. Then he spat on the used stamp and massaged it with his fingertip until it came loose. It lifted off the envelope clean as a whistle.

"There's still glue on it," he said. "Maybe it'll stick." It stuck nicely. "But it's got to look like it's been franked."

"I got an idea." Matthew licked his fingertip, rubbed it on the sole of his shoe until it was dirty, then he carefully smudged the stamp.

"That's flippin' good," approved Graham, and Matthew grinned.

Just then they heard Flossie and Auntie Murna come back from shopping. Flossie always brought the post in and put it on the hall table.

Graham crept down the stairs, slipped Matthew's letter in the middle of the pile, and crept back up again.

They waited until they heard Mother Button whistling "I've got sixpence . . ." which meant she was finished her work and was in good humour again. Then they strolled casually downstairs together.

Mother Button was in the hall shuffling through the letters. "What's this, then?" she said.

Both boys stopped on the landing, holding their breath, as Mother Button held the envelope at arm's length because she didn't have her reading glasses on. "It's for you, Matthew." She handed it to him without a hint of suspicion and took the rest of the mail into the sitting room.

Heaving a sigh of relief, they ripped open the envelope and read their forgery. Then they took it into the sitting room where Mother Button was smiling at a postcard. "My cousin Maude (the boys pulled a funny face at the name Maude) is having a lovely holiday in Yarmouth," she remarked.

Then Matthew handed her the letter. She read it through twice. "What a nice invitation," she said. "But I'm sorry, Matthew, I can't afford to send you."

"Oh, I can pay my own way," Matthew said. "I've saved all the money I've earned this summer."

"And what friend would you like to take with you, Tony or Tom?" teased Mother Button.

Putting his skinny arm around Graham's sturdy shoulders, he said, "I'm taking my mate."

Chapter 9

Visit to Ipswich

It was a forty-minute journey by train to Ipswich. From the Railway Station they boarded a green trolley bus marked "Cornhill." The trolley bus had two poles connected to overhead wires that made a high, singing noise as the bus travelled along.

Graham had never felt so carefree and happy in his life. "It's a lot more fun," he thought, "having a mate to share an adventure with."

On the way to town the trolley bus passed a huge pile of rubble behind a high wire fence. Broken teeter-totters and swings were sticking up out of the pile. Graham leaned out the window to see. "I didn't know Ipswich got bombed, Matty. I thought it was mostly London," he said.

"Oh, no, the Jerries blasted us too. That used to be a school back there."

"What happened to it?"

"It was a direct hit by a doodlebug." A doodlebug was a buzz bomb, like a pilotless plane.

"Cor! Did anybody get killed?"

"No. Lucky it was Sunday and the school was closed."

They got off at the town centre. Around the perimeter of the cobblestone square were the central post office, the town hall and lots of shops and pubs. Peter's Ice Cream Cart was pedalling around the square so they treated themselves to cones, one chocolate and one strawberry.

Sitting on a wooden bench, they licked their ice creams as fast as they melted in the hot August sun and watched the people strolling by.

"Have you got a picture of your mum?" asked Matthew.

"Only up here." Graham tapped his forehead.

"How will you recognize her then?"

"I'll know her when I see her."

Popping the last tip of the cone into his mouth Graham said, "Okay, mate, let's go."

Again he walked right up to strange ladies and asked if their name was Robbertson with two b's. But it was the same as in London. Some were nice and some were nasty and nobody's name was Robbertson. They strolled along Tavern Street and stopped in front of the White Horse Hotel. There was a statue of a white stallion prancing over the door.

"Charles Dickens stayed here once," Matthew told Graham. "I've got one of his books in my case. I'll lend it . . ." Suddenly he grabbed Graham's arm. "There's a lady looks like you," he said. The lady was window-shopping at Croydon's Jewellery Store. Graham studied her reflection in the glass. She was quite a young woman, stockily built, wearing a blue print dress. Her bobbed brown hair was cut in a fringe across her forehead.

Graham wiped his own fringe sideways with a sweaty palm. Then he walked right up to her. "Excuse me," he said and she turned to him with a smile. "She's got a pretty smile," he thought, his heart fluttering, "and her eyes are the colour of hazelnuts, just like mine!"

"Would your name happen to be Mrs. Robbertson?" he asked.

"How did you ever guess?" she gasped in surprise.

His heart was beating as fast as a hummingbird's wings. "Because you look like a Mrs. Robbertson I know," he said "Is your name spelled with two b's?"

"No, it's spelled with one. Why do you ask?"

"Well, the lady I'm looking for is Mrs. Robbertson with two b's," he said, his heart slowing down now with disappointment.

"I hope you find her, then," she said and waved goodbye as she pushed through Croydon's double doors.

They sat down on another bench. "Maybe your name is spelled wrong on your birth certificate," suggested Matthew.

"No." Graham gave his head a shake. "Birth certificates don't have mistakes on them. But I'm tired of looking today. Why don't we find your relations? Do you know where they live?"

"Yes. Twenty Lambeth Lane. But I'm not sure I want to go there anymore."

"Why not?" Graham tried not to sound too curious.

"Well . . . they might not want to see me after all."

"What makes you think that?" asked Graham.

"If I tell you, you got to swear to secrecy," Matthew said.

"I swear," agreed Graham.

So they spit on their hands and shook and sealed their second secret.

"Well, my mother ran off to Australia with the gas man and left me with my aunt and uncle. And they didn't want me neither. So they sent me to Mother Button's." He sighed and shrugged his bony shoulders. "I don't think they even like me. Nobody likes me."

"I like you, mate," Graham said.

Matthew's skinny face stretched in a wide grin. "I like you, too, mate."

They laughed and Graham jumped up off the bench. "Anyway, maybe they've changed their minds about you. Let's go find out."

Matthew knew what bus to take to Lambeth Lane, and in fifteen minutes they were standing outside a red brick house with green shutters and lace curtains on a bay window.

Matthew hung back, so Graham pushed open the iron garden gate and prodded his mate up the short walk.

"Knock on the door," he said.

Matthew knocked but nobody came.

"Hey, did you see that curtain move? Knock again," urged Graham. "Knock hard this time."

Matthew knocked till his knuckles turned red but still nobody came.

"I think we better go." Matthew's mouth twitched nervously.

"Why don't you try the back door, Matty? Maybe nobody heard you."

So they followed a pebbled path around the house to the back door. On the window of the back door was a flimsy muslin curtain they could see through. Matthew stood on tiptoe on the doorstep and cupped his hands around his eyes and pressed his nose against the pane. "I can see her," he whispered.

"Who?" hissed Graham.

"My auntie."

"What's she doing?"

"Sitting at the table."

"Well, rap on the glass," urged Graham. "If she was in the back all along she probably didn't hear you out the front."

Matthew rapped, rat-a-tat-tat, as he peered through the curtain. "Uh-oh," he said.

"Uh-oh, what?"

"She looked right at me. I'm sure she saw me. Uh-oh! She jumped up and ran down the hall. She's gone."

He stepped away from the door and heaved a big sigh. "I guess she hasn't changed her mind about me after all," he said.

Graham looked at his friend and saw tears in his eyes. "Ah, give over, mate. Don't blubber. She ain't worth it. Let's go home."

They retraced their steps. Matthew went through the gate with his head down and didn't look back. But Graham darted one more glance at the front window. A corner of the lace curtain was pinched back and he caught a glimpse of a boy's face. Anger for Matthew's sake flared up inside him like a roman candle. Grabbing the gate, he flung it shut so hard that the whole fence shook and rattled. Then he raced past Matthew to the bus stop, hollering, "Last one there's a horsefly!"

Chapter 10

The Third Search

Graham wasn't very disappointed with the fruitless search. He hadn't really expected to find his mother in Ipswich. He was still convinced she lived in London. But hadn't they had a grand day in Ipswich before they went to Lambeth Lane? It had been great fun being on the loose with Matthew. And the best part was that they weren't in any trouble when they got home.

They had spent all their money on train fare and treats so Graham was anxious to earn more. He had found out how badly you needed money to travel: not having to sneak onto trains and steal bread rolls and worry about being pounced on by the police made all the difference in the world.

"Have you got any more jobs we can do?" he asked Mother Button the very next day.

"Don't tell me you spent every penny in Ipswich?" she said, sounding a bit suspicious.

"Well, we treated everybody," he boasted. "We bought all Matty's cousins ice-cream cones and chewing gum."

"Well, that was mighty generous of you." Mother Button swallowed the story, hook, line and sinker. "I've always said you were a good boy."

"She did, she always said that. I heard her with my own ears," repeated Auntie Murna as she wiped tears from her eyes with the corner of her apron. She was slicing onions for scalloped potatoes.

Graham gave his shoulders a guilty little shrug.

"I wonder," said Mother Button, "if you and Matthew could handle a paint job?"

"I know how to paint," interrupted Tony Scooter. He and Tom had got fired from their summer jobs for messing about. "Me and Tom can do it. You need us big boys for that job."

"I don't trust you two as far as I can throw you," Mother Button snapped at Tony. "Besides, everything the two of you do is slapdash. I don't want my garden furniture to be done slapdash."

"Mother asked us first," said Graham, elbowing Tony aside. He wasn't the least bit afraid of Tony anymore. Ever since he had stuck up for Matthew and Tony had backed down, he had come to realize that bullies were just cowards in disguise.

So Graham and Matthew got the paint job. There were two wicker armchairs, a wicker lounger and a round wooden table to paint.

"We'll start on the chairs," Graham said.

They changed into old clothes and set to work. The white paint went on as smooth as icing on a cake. They worked happily together the whole afternoon and by four o'clock they were both dripping sweat. It was an extra-hot morning, even for mid-August.

Flossie came out on the back step waving her arms like wings to create a breeze in her armpits. "Time for dinner boys, come on in," she said. Then she added. "You're doing a lovely job." Only the round table was left to paint.

Graham stomped the lid on the gallon bucket with the heel of his boot, and Matthew put the brushes to soak in a pint jar of turpentine.

The other boys were already eating. Graham could hear the clicking of spoons on plates. Mother didn't allow talking and eating at the same time. She had a strict code of manners. Graham and Matthew washed up quickly at the scullery sink and slipped into their chairs.

For dinner they had mutton chops, scalloped potatoes and mushy green peas. Graham hated mushy peas. He wished Auntie Murna wouldn't mash them.

Matthew took one look at his plate and whispered, "I can't eat this stuff."

"You eat it up, now." Mother had overheard him. "And don't waste a drop of that water. It's full of vit-a-mins, you know." The vegetable water was green as grass from garden peas.

"I can't," whispered Matthew putting down his spoon.

"You got to or she won't let you leave the table," reminded Graham. "Shovel them in quick and then wash them down with the water."

Squeezing his eyes shut, Matthew opened his mouth and began shovelling.

"Oh, see how Matty loves his mushies," sneered Tony from the other side of the table.

"Let's give him more then," hissed Tom. Mother had her back turned so they both reached across the table and slopped their peas onto Matthew's plate.

All around the table the boys were snickering behind their hands. Then, just as Mother and Flossie sat down at either end of the table, Matthew threw up. Slime as green as grass spewed out of his mouth across the snow-white tablecloth.

The big boys jumped up, knocking over their chairs; the little boys squawked and squealed and Flossie and Mother leapt, gagging, to their feet. Then Matthew slid quietly off the chair and disappeared under the table.

"God save us, he's fainted!" cried Mother Button, her hand flying to her throat.

"I'll get him," cried Flossie. Graham helped her pull him out from under the table and carry him up to bed. They mounted the stairs, Flossie at Matthew's armpits and Graham at his feet. "He's light as a goose-feather," Graham thought. They laid him gently on top of the bed-spread.

Mother came hurrying after them with a basin of water. "There, there," she murmured as she bathed Matthew's head and wiped around his mouth. Flossie ran back down and brought up another basin of fresh water and a clean flannel and a bottle of smelling-salts. But Matthew didn't need the smelling-salts. He had come to on his own. He moaned softly and his eyes flickered open.

"What happened?" he asked in a raspy whisper.

"Don't talk now, love, save your strength," Mother said. Wringing out the flannel, Mother folded it into a pad and placed it on his forehead. "Auntie Murna's gone for Doctor Gosden. He'll soon put you right," she said soothingly.

When Matthew was cleaned up and resting on the pillows, Graham sat beside him on the bed. "Don't worry, mate," he said. "You'll be right as rain tomorrow." But Graham wondered. He had never seen a face so white. White as bread dough. Even whiter . . . more like snow.

"We have to finish our paint job," gasped Matthew.

"Don't worry, Matty. We'll finish tomorrow," Graham said.

Just then Auntie Murna ushered the doctor in and Mother sent Graham out of the room. "You can come back later," she promised.

Downstairs, the soiled white tablecloth had been replaced by a clean checkered one. On it was a plate of cheese and biscuits and a glass bowl of blue plums. But the sick smell was still in the air and the boys had lost their appetites. Flossie gave them permission to leave the table and they all ran outside for fresh air.

All except Graham. He hung around the kitchen. Auntie Murna was bent over the sink washing new-laid eggs. Graham noticed her crooked fingers were trembling. So he picked up the tea towel and began drying the eggs, one by one, and putting them in a wire basket on the table. He wanted to ask Auntie Murna about Matty . . . how sick was he? Was he sick enough to die? But he couldn't get the words past the hard lump in his throat.

Chapter 11

Matthew

"He's a very sick boy." Dr. Gosden's kind face was lined with concern. "What he needs now is complete bed rest and constant care. Perhaps I could arrange for him to go to the convalescent home. Unless there's someone here can nurse him."

Mother Button shook her head and brushed a strand of hair out of her eyes. There's grey in her hair, Graham noticed for the first time. She must be getting old. At least 46 or maybe even 50. Not old like Auntie Murna, of course. He couldn't even guess how old Auntie Murna might be.

"I've got ten boys right now," Mother Button explained to the doctor, wringing her hands. "And ten rooms to clean. And a new little fellow coming soon. I don't think I could manage." She looked at Auntie Murna, sitting dejectedly by the cooker, her humped back sticking out like a broken wing under her black dress. "And Murna's not fit for nursing," she said.

"Perhaps I could do it," said Flossie. Standing up, she

towered over her mother and the doctor. "I'm young and strong."

"I'll help Flossie look after Matty," volunteered Graham. Then he added, as if it might make a difference, "He's my mate."

"Well, Missus." Dr. Gosden picked up his black bag. "I'll leave the boy in your capable hands for now. But I'll be back." He took out the pocket watch that hung on a gold chain looped across his stomach, glanced at the time and hurried down the hall to the front door.

When the door had closed behind him Graham looked around to see if any of the other boys were within earshot. They were nowhere in sight so he sidled up to Mother Button. "Did the doctor say what's wrong with Matty?" he asked.

"He said Matthew's heart is weak, probably from rheumatic fever," she answered with a sigh. "And the garden work was too much for him, poor lad. If I'd known I'd never have let him do it."

"But will he get better?" persisted Graham. "If I do his share of the work, will he get better?"

"The Lord only knows, Graham. We'll have to wait and see, won't we?"

* * *

For two weeks Flossie never left Matthew's side. And Mother Button put a spare mattress on the floor for Graham to sleep on so that Matthew could have the bed all to himself.

Every waking moment Graham was there to do Flossie's bidding: up and down the stairs he ran, fetching water and mustard plasters and helping Flossie turn Matthew over so he wouldn't get bedsores. Then twice a day Mother Button sent him up with her own homemade tonic: a mixture of malt and molasses and cod-liver oil. Graham was the only one who could coax Matthew to open his mouth and swallow the nasty tasting stuff.

Two weeks went by and the good doctor came every day. Slowly Matthew began to improve. At the end of the second week, as he folded up his stethoscope and tucked it into his black bag, Dr. Gosden said, "Today, young man, I'm going to let you sit out in the garden."

"Oh, lovely!" Flossie clapped her hands. Flossie had proved to be a wonderful nurse for Matthew. "Graham, love, will you get the sun-lounger out from the shelter and set it up under the apple tree? And I'll get a blanket and pillow to make it comfy."

When Matthew was propped up on the lounger Graham said, "How would you like a game of chess, Matty? Do you think you're up to beating me?"

Matthew gave him a wan smile. "I'll give it a go, mate," he said.

So every day for a week Graham set the chessboard up on a wooden tray across Matthew's lap. But Matthew played listlessly and Graham cried "checkmate" over and over again.

"It's no fun if you let me win," Graham complained.

"I'm not letting you win, mate, you're getting good!"

Just then Flossie came to the door. "Graham," she said with her bright pearly smile, "Miss Featherstone just rang. She wants you to drop by her house. She says she's got a job for you."

Miss Featherstone! He hadn't seen his teacher since the start of the holiday. "Will you be all right, Matty? Shall I help you into the house?"

"I can manage by myself," Matthew said shortly.

"You don't mind if I go, then?"

"No. Course not. I've got my book to read." Matthew was reading *Treasure Island*. When he had been too sick to read to himself Graham had read to him out loud. At first Graham was embarrassed because he made mistakes and stumbled over big words, but Matthew taught him what each one meant and once he knew the word Graham never forgot it. Matthew said he had a photographic memory.

Chapter 12

Miss Featherstone's House

The teacher lived in a thatched cottage with two dormer windows. A wood-shingled roof peaked over the front door. Just as he was about to knock she came around the corner of the house and Graham caught his breath.

She was wearing a sky-blue dress that matched her eyes. And her dark hair, which she wore in a plain roll around her head in school, fell out from under her wide straw hat in shiny black waves. The sight of her made Graham's heart skip beats.

"Hello, Miss Featherstone," he said breathlessly.

"Well, hello Graham!" She peeled off her yellow garden gloves and held out her hand. It felt soft and smooth.

"Flossie said you wanted me," he said shyly.

"Come along and we'll talk about it over lemonade," she said.

She led him on a flagstone path to the back of the house. In the middle of the back garden was a round summerhouse hemmed in by shrubs and flowers. "This is my retreat," she said. "My favourite summer spot."

The summerhouse was woven, like a big basket, of natural-coloured wood and the furniture inside was black wrought iron. "Make yourself at home," said Miss Featherstone. Then she went inside her cottage. He wondered if she lived alone in there. He knew she wasn't married because she was still called Miss. If she was married she would be Missus, wouldn't she?

She came back with a painted tray and set it on the table. On it were two tall tumblers of lemonade and a plate of digestive biscuits. Bits of lemon floated in the lemonade and yellow wedges clung to the glass rims. Graham watched as Miss Featherstone squeezed her wedge into her drink and dropped it in with a little plunk. So he did the same. Then he took a long, slow sip. He'd never tasted anything more delicious.

"Aaah!" he breathed, smacking his lips.

Her blue eyes twinkled as she pushed the plate across the table. "Help yourself to a digestive," she said. "Take as many as you like."

He ate three in a row.

"Well, now, tell me a little bit about yourself, Graham. For instance, how did you come to live at Velma Villa?"

"Umm, well, when I was a tiny baby, only three weeks old, my mother left me at the Home for Unwanteds. And I stayed there until I was six years old. Then I got sent to Mother Button's. And I'm glad I did because Mother Button is good to us boys."

"I'm glad to hear that." Miss Featherstone nodded approvingly. "Tell me more about yourself. Do you have another name besides Graham?"

"Oh, yes. On my birth certificate it says my name is

Neill Graham Robbertson. Neill has two l's."

"Your mother must have loved you very much to give you such a distinguished name," she said.

"Do you think so? I never thought of that."

She began stacking the dishes on the tray. "And the other ladies at Velma Villa, what are they like?"

"Oh, they're nice, too. Flossie is Mother's daughter. She's nearly grown up and she's got a boyfriend. He takes her to the picture house on Saturday nights."

"And the other lady . . . the one you call Auntie Murna?"

"Oh, she's a good one, Auntie Murna is. She saved my life once, you know."

"No, I didn't know, tell me about it."

"Well, one day, when I was only seven or eight, I forget which, I decided to make Mother afternoon tea. So I climbed up on a chair and turned on the gas jet and lit it with a match just like I'd seen Mother do. Well, the flame shot out and caught my shirt on fire. I screamed my head off and Auntie Murna came running and beat out the flames with her bare hands. Then she threw me into the old baby pram that we cart groceries in and she pushed me all the way to the hospital. We both had bad burns, me on my stomach and Auntie Murna on her hands. Do you want to see my scars?" He undid a button of his shirt.

"Some other time." She gave a little shudder. "Now tell me what you've been doing with yourself all summer long. Have you been staying out of mischief?"

"Yes, I have, because I've been helping Flossie take care of Matthew," he said, doing up the button. "Matty's got a weak heart, you know; Mother thinks he got it from rheumatic fever. He took bad after me and him painted the garden furniture. At dinner that night we had mushy peas and green water and . . ."

"Green water?"

"Yes, from the peas. Mother always makes us drink our vegetable water because it's chock full of vit-a-mins. She says that's why us Home boys are so healthy. But Matty was already sick but Mother didn't know it. And he threw up green slime all over the table. Then he fainted and fell off the chair. You shoulda smelled it Miss. Oh, it was awful."

The teacher's face turned pale as paper. She covered her mouth with her hand. "Don't say another word, Graham," she begged.

"I'm sorry, Miss Featherstone."

"That's all right. Now let's get down to business. How would you like to cut my grass and trim my shrubs and nip my flowers? And how does half a crown a week sound to you for the rest of the growing season?"

Half a crown a week! "It sounds grand," he said. "When can I start?"

"Right now," she said, picking up the tray.

He spent the rest of the afternoon weeding and trimming and nipping. And by the end of the week the back garden and the shrubs around the cottage door, looked like a picture in Mother's *Home and Garden* magazine.

"It's never looked so lovely," Miss Featherstone said as she handed him the half-crown.

Glowing with pride, he ran all the way home.

Chapter 13

The Promise

That night he showed the half-crown to Matthew. Mother had sent Matthew to bed early because he was still recuperating. Graham was tired, too, from gardening, so he climbed in beside him. The other boys had not come upstairs yet.

"What are you going to do with it, mate?" asked Matthew, his hazel eyes burning bright above his hollow cheekbones.

"I'm off to London," Graham whispered.

"Can I come with you, Gray?"

"Not this time, Matty. Wait till you're stronger." Graham raised up on his elbow and looked Matthew straight in the eye. "When Mother asks you where I went, what are you going to say?"

"Ummm . . . that you went to see my cousin Rodney?"

"Great, Matty. You're a real pal."

Graham leaned back on his pillow and clasped his hands behind his head. He heard Matthew's breathing become soft in sleep. So he closed his own eyes and drifted off.

He woke up when the clock in the parlour struck four. Graham eased himself out of bed; then he crouched on the floor to lace on his shoes so as not to disturb Matthew. He was already dressed because he'd gone to bed with his clothes again.

"Don't get lost in the fog," came Matthew's thin whisper. Graham reached across the bed and squeezed his friend's bony fingers. "Don't worry mate, I won't. I know London like the back of my hand," he bragged.

"Will you promise me something, mate?" Matthew's voice was soft and breathy.

"Anything, Matty."

"Promise me you'll never give up."

"Oh, I promise that for sure, Matty." Very quietly he spit on his hand and Matty did the same and they sealed another secret.

Then he tiptoed past the three narrow beds where Tony and Tom and Benny-the-bulldog were sawing wood (which is what Mother called snoring) and crept down the stairs, carefully missing the squeaky board. He let himself out of the house without a sound.

Then he had to wait at the station for the six a.m. train. He proudly paid his fare. No more sneaking onto trains for Graham Robbertson!

* * *

London! How he loved the big bustling city. No matter how early in the morning, London was wide awake and busy as a beehive.

"First I'll have breakfast," Graham thought, jingling the coins in his pocket. Besides the half-crown, he had a pocketful of change. He hadn't spent a penny while he was helping care for Matthew, and he felt rich as that American bloke, Rockefeller.

He stopped for breakfast at Liverpool Street Station: scrambled eggs and tea and toast. Then he headed for the marketplace, Covent Garden. The smell of apples and oranges lured him over to a loaded fruit stall. He bought one of each and ate them on the spot. Then, ducking in and out between the stalls, he asked dozens of lady shoppers if their name was Robbertson. But the answer was always the same, "NO!"

Discouraged, he decided to ride the bright red double-deckers instead of taking the Underground, so that he could see more people on the street. He got a front seat on the open upper deck and rode for hours all over the city. From up there he saw lots of ladies bustling in and out of shops, who might have been his mother. But in the time it took to scramble down the spiral staircase the bus always started up again. So he got off at Trafalgar Square. He dashed across the pavement to the foot of the monument, scattering flocks of screaming pigeons. Craning his neck, he nearly fell over backwards staring up at Admiral Lord Nelson. The statue was so high on top the tall cement column that a pigeon perched on the Admiral's head looked like a tiny white fly.

His stomach had begun to grumble. "It must be lunchtime," he thought. And sure enough the clock above the Lord Nelson's Pub struck twelve. Looking in the open pub door he saw that it was full of smoke and noisy men. A man on a stool by the door was tucking into a hot sausage sandwich. Opening his mouth wide, he took a huge bite and brown sauce squeezed out the corners of his mouth onto his red beard. The sight made Graham drool. But he knew boys weren't allowed in pubs, so he went into the cafe next door.

When the waiter came Graham said, "Do you have sausage sandwiches like they got next door?" And to his surprise the waiter said yes, they had. So Graham ordered it up with a bottle of ginger beer.

Chapter 14

Hooligans

He left the caff feeling good and ran across the square to the fountain. Just for fun, he stood perfectly still like Nelson's statue and held out his arms. A flock of pigeons rose up in a cloud and landed all over him. Then Graham spun around, his arms flapping like wings, sending the birds screeching into the air.

On the other side of the square stood a long grey building called The National Gallery. "I wonder what's in there?" he thought. "I bet Matty would know." He missed Matthew. "I hope he's better next time so he can come with me."

Stopping at a newsstand on the corner he picked up a city map. "How much, please?" he asked the newsman whose weathered face was wrinkled like a dried apple. "Tuppence," the man said with a toothless grin. So Graham gave him tuppence and sat on a bench at the bus stop to study the map.

Turning it over, he found the outline of the Underground. The lines were all different colours, according to where you wanted to go: green and brown and blue and yellow and red and black. With the stub of a pencil he had in his pocket, Graham crossed out the places he'd already been. Then he picked the green line because it looked the longest. Following the crowd into the station he paid his fare and pushed through the turnstile.

He stepped on an escalator that was so long and deep, the people at the bottom looked like scurrying ants. "No wonder it's called the Underground," he thought, clinging to the moving handrail.

The train came roaring through the tube and screeched to a stop. Graham hopped on the nearest car. It went rattling through the tunnels at breathtaking speed. After an hour's ride, swaying back and forth, Graham began to feel queasy. He burped and tasted the sausage sandwich. His stomach rumbled and he began breaking wind again.

The woman beside him held a hanky to her nose and darted him a suspicious look. So he leaped off at the next stop and got on another long escalator going up. Up wasn't so bad. Coming out into the sunlight he took a big gulp of fresh air. His stomach settled with a gurgle and the last of the wind escaped. In his mind he could hear Mother Button saying, "Better to toot and bear the shame, than not to toot and bear the pain!" He laughed and felt himself excused.

The sign on the station wall said GAINSBOROUGH. He'd never heard of the place so he decided to scout around. There wasn't much to see in Gainsborough, just a few shops and crumbling churches. The town centre was a boarded-up square. Loud noises came from behind the boards and people were looking through knotholes. So Graham found a knothole his height and peeked through it. Big cranes and lorries and men with picks and shovels were tearing down brick walls and clearing away piles of rubble. Another scary reminder of the Blitz.

Walking away Graham thought, "One good thing about being an orphan . . . you can't lose nobody in the war if you don't have nobody, can you?" He knew Mother Button had lost a younger brother named Walter, and Auntie Murna was still mourning a missing grandson. "Only eighteen years old, he was," she'd say with a terrible sigh. So November the eleventh was a day of deep mourning at Velma Villa.

Graham sauntered around Gainsborough for hours, but he didn't see any women that even remotely resembled the picture he carried in his mind of his mother. The only interesting person he saw was a G.I. There were still a few American soldiers about. He remembered hearing a Yankee song on the wireless during the war: "Over there! Over there! Oh, the Yanks are comin', the Yanks are comin', and we won't be back till it's over over there!"

"You were bloomin' late comin'," Graham thought. "And now it's over why don't you go home?" But the G.I. gave him a cheery grin, so Graham said, "Got any gum, chum?" Americans were well known for always having gum in their pockets.

"Sure, chum, here you are." The Yankee gave him a full pack of Wrigley's Spearmint and Graham said thanks very much.

Folding two sticks into his mouth at once — lovely flavour, spearmint — he saw a red telephone kiosk outside a chemist's shop. He went inside and opened the thin directory to the letter R. He was amazed to find two Robbertsons with two b's, so he memorized the addresses: 22 King Road and 14 Peter Street.

He found them both easily since Gainsborough was such a small place. Number 22 King Road was a little cottage with a thatched roof. But it wasn't pretty like Miss Featherstone's. It had ragged holes in the thatch where birds had made their nests. He knocked on the front door which was so small it looked like a dollhouse door.

An old man with a humped back like Auntie Murna's creaked open the door. He looked excited, as if it was a rare treat for someone to knock on his door.

"Have you ever heard of a lady by the name of Marietta Robbertson?" Graham asked. Then he thought, "If the answer is yes, maybe he's my grandfather."

The old man frowned and wagged his head. "Nah, can't say that I have. But I'll ask my old dutch." Turning, he called over his shoulder, "Jenny! You there. This young fella is looking for somebody by the name of . . ." he raised his ragged eyebrows questioningly.

"Marietta Robbertson," repeated Graham.

His old dutch, who turned out to be his wife, was as bent as he was. She waggled her stringy grey head. "Never in all me life," she said.

So he thanked them both and asked what time it was. The man squinted at his pocket watch and said, "It's half-four, nigh on teatime. Goodbye to you, then," and he shut the door.

Next, Graham looked for 14 Peter Street. It was a run-down clapboard house with weeds as tall as hay crowding around the door. The man who answered his knock was unshaven and bleary-eyed and when Graham asked him the question the man told him to push off.

"Same to you, old goat!" Graham snapped back.

Then he made a mad dash for the tube station and thankfully boarded a train. Changing lines several times just for fun, he finally emerged from underground, like a mole, at Leicester Square. The first thing he smelled was chips! Fish and chips!

The lovely smell was coming from an open chip shop on the square. A man with a rag tied around his head like a pirate was lifting a batch of chips out of the bubbling fat.

"Cod and chips, please," Graham said. "Three penny-worth." He paid with his last bit of change. Then he went across the street to a little park and found himself a nice private bench under a holly bush.

"Yum," he murmured to himself as he munched on the fish and chips, smothered in salt and vinegar. "Mmm, yum." He stuffed a crunchy golden chip as long as his middle finger into his mouth.

Lost in the pleasure of the lovely flavours, he failed to notice, until it was too late, that two big boys, much bigger than Tony and Tom, had crept up behind the holly bush. Pouncing on him like snarling dogs, one hit him over the head with something hard and the other began tearing at his clothes. He tried to scream but he couldn't because two rough hands had a stranglehold around his throat. The last thing he remembered was the sound of his pocket ripping, then a blinding pain and blackness settling over him like a blanket.

* * *

He woke up slowly to find his head cradled in a lady's lap.

As her face came into focus he saw that she had a soft brown fringe across her forehead, hazel eyes and a sweet smile. "Are you my mother?" he asked in a croaky whisper.

"No, my dear, but I live nearby and I'm going to take you home. I've called for a policeman. Oh, here he is now."

The bobby leaned over Graham and asked him questions. Graham told him what had happened the best he could but he couldn't describe the faces of the hooligans.

"He's got a lump on his head the size of a goose egg," the lady said. "Not much wonder he can't remember." She touched his crown, gingerly, where his hair stuck up like a feather and her hand came away with blood on her fingers.

"Can you stand up, lad?" asked the policeman.

"I think so." They helped him to his feet and the world began spinning like a top. Through a dizzy haze he saw a flock of pigeons fighting over the remains of his supper.

At the police station he had to repeat everything he could remember and the bobby wrote it down.

A throbbing pain in his head made him wince and squeeze his eyes shut.

"Can I take him home now, officer?" the lady asked anxiously.

"Are you his mother?" he queried.

"No, no, just a friend. But I'd like to help."

"Well, he needs to get that head stitched up. But we'll have to call his family first. Someone has to sign for the surgery."

Graham's first thought was, not what Mother Button would do, but what would Miss Featherstone think of him now?

The nice lady who looked like his mother kissed him goodbye and whispered in his ear, "My name is Mrs. Virginia Temple. If you're ever in London again, look me up. I live at 47 Aston Road, in Bayswater."

Then Graham was loaded into a Black Maria and taken home to Bury St. Edmunds.

Chapter 15

Punishment Postponed

This scolding was the worst ever.

"He won't need stitches." Mother parted his hair none too gently and examined the cut on his head. "I've attended lots worse than this."

"Then I'll leave him in your capable hands, Madam." The bobby touched his helmet and left.

"Sit on that chair," ordered Mother Button. Graham sat and clung to the edge of the seat; he winced in pain as she cleaned the gash.

"Owww!" he cried when she doused it with iodine. "You're hurting me!"

"That's nothing to what you deserve, young man," she railed, winding a bandage, roughly, around his head. "So you went to visit Matthew's cousin Rodney, did you? Now isn't it strange you should be brought home in a London Black Maria when you've spent the day in Ipswich? And the shame of it is, you got that poor sick boy to lie for you. Well, you'll pay for it — I can promise you that. Tomorrow I'll decide what's to be done with you. Now get upstairs to bed and don't you dare disturb Matthew. He's worse today and not much wonder."

Matthew was alone in the room. Tony and Tom and Benny-the-bulldog had gone to the pictures again. Undressing quietly, Graham crept into bed. His head was aching so badly he had to grit his teeth to keep from crying out, and he didn't dare ask Mother for an aspirin tablet.

Just then the door eased opened and Flossie tiptoed in. She placed a cold compress on his head and slipped out again.

"She's a good one, isn't she?" whispered Matthew.

"Matty! You're awake. Are you all right, mate?"

Instead of answering Matthew said, "I want you to promise me something, Gray."

"Anything, Matty. You name it."

"Promise you won't run off again without me."

Graham hesitated. How long would it take for Matty to get strong enough to travel? he wondered.

"Are you going to promise?" Matthew's voice was thin as thread, but it demanded an answer.

"All right, Matty, I promise."

Then, his voice fading, Matthew said, "I'm sorry, mate."

"It's not you that needs to be sorry, Matty, it's me. But are you all right?"

When Matthew answered, Graham heard a rattle in his chest. "I'm dead scared," Matthew whispered.

Reaching across the blanket Graham gripped his friend's bony fingers. "Don't be scared, Matty."

No answer, just whispery breathing. Graham thought he had fallen asleep.

Then, in a voice so weak Graham could hardly hear, Matthew said, "Never give up, mate."

"I never will, Matty."

Then Matthew fell asleep again.

Graham lay perfectly still, flat on his back the cold compress easing the pain away. "What will happen to me this time?" he asked himself? At last, he fell asleep.

Chapter 16

The Middle of the Night

Graham woke with a sudden start. Reaching up he felt his head through the bandage. The goose egg was still there and it hurt to touch. He swallowed and his throat was raw where the fingers had dug into his neck. His body hurt all over from the beating he'd got in Leicester Square.

He sighed, thankful that he was safe in bed beside Matthew even though he dreaded the morning.

He drifted in and out of sleep but the loud snores from across the room kept waking him. Tony and Tom both snored like sailors and Benny-the-bulldog growled in his sleep, but it had never bothered Graham before. Suddenly he felt a strange sensation, like spiders creeping all over his body.

Turning his sore head slowly on the pillow, he whispered, "Matty!" No answer. Not a sound.

Walking his fingers across the cover he found Matthew's hand. It was ice cold. He leapt out of bed, pain ripping at his body, and snapped on the light. The three big boys went right on snoring. Creeping back to the bedside he leaned over and looked closely at Matthew. His face was the colour of waxed paper; his eyes were half open; his mouth was half open, too, baring his teeth in a gruesome grin. His lips were navy blue.

"MATTY!" Graham turned and ran screaming into the hallway. "MOTHER! FLOSSIE! AUNTIE MURNA! COME QUICK!"

His screams woke the whole house. Hallway doors flew open and the three women came running in their nightclothes.

"What's the matter? Whatcha yelling about?" complained Tony, rubbing his eyes.

"Stupid Stinker," grumbled Tom burying his head under the pillow.

"Grrrr!" growled the Bulldog.

"Be quiet, all of you!" snapped Mother Button. Leaning over the bed she bent her ear to Matthew's blue lips. Then she lifted his thin wrist between her thumb and finger. His hand hung as limp as an empty glove. Tenderly, Mother put it down by his side and drew the cover up over his face.

"He's gone, poor little lad," she whispered.

* * *

Matthew Penny's funeral was held at the Congregational Church on Whiting Street. The plain white coffin was open, sitting on a trestle in front of the altar. Flossie had arranged flowers from the garden at the head and foot of the casket.

Graham was allowed to sit in the front pew on the left side of the aisle with Mother Button and Flossie and Auntie Murna. On the right side Matthew's Ipswich relations were lined up in a row: his uncle, two aunts and his cousin Rodney. Graham recognized the face he had seen at the window on Lattice Lane. He hated Rodney on sight.

Reverend Edgar Foreman walked quietly up the aisle and looked down at the frail little person in the coffin. He bowed his head in silent prayer. Then he turned to the people. "Does anyone wish to say a final farewell?" He spoke mainly to the front row of mourners.

The relatives all got up and hovered around the coffin. The two aunts patted their eyes with their hankies. Rodney and his father gazed down at the dead boy.

"They don't even like me." Graham heard Matty's voice, plain as day, in his head.

"Do you want to say a last goodbye?" whispered Flossie.

"No." Graham glared at the relatives. "I want to kill them."

"Shhh!" whispered Mother Button.

Then Rev. Foreman gently closed the coffin lid and Matthew Penny disappeared forever.

After the burial the mourners were invited back to Velma Villa for refreshments. A lovely repast had been provided by the neighbours. Even Mr. Beetle had contributed two sponge cakes and a tin of Blue Bird Biscuits. In the middle of the table sat the biggest basket of fruit Graham had ever seen. A card tied to the basket's handle read, "In loving sympathy from Miss Featherstone."

Everybody, especially Matthew's relatives, seemed to be thoroughly enjoying themselves. But Graham was feeling sick with guilt and sorrow.

"Won't you have a little bite, love?" asked Auntie

Murna, offering him the plate of biscuits.

"I'm not hungry," he said. Then he excused himself and went outside to the shelter. Shutting the door behind him he slid down into a dark corner and burst into tears.

It wasn't until that night, the night of the funeral, that Graham realized that three days had passed since Matthew had died and not another word had been said about his latest escapade to London.

Chapter 17

The New Boy

Graham only had the double bed all to himself for two nights when an eight-year-old boy by the name of Billy Tree arrived at Velma Villa and the only place for him to sleep was Matthew's half of the bed.

Graham hated having a new bedmate. "When I grow up," he promised himself, "I'm going to have a double bed all to my ownself and I'll never share it with nobody." Then he thought, "but what if I get married?" He sometimes daydreamed about being a grown man with a wife and children. Then he'd have a family of his own, and he could stop looking for his mother.

His thoughts were interrupted by Billy returning from the bathroom for the third time that night. On his way back the little boy bumped into all three beds on the opposite side of the room.

"Hey you, Bumper!" said Tony. "Watch where you're going or I'll give you what for."

Billy Tree had already earned himself the nickname of Bumper because he bumped into everything: the table and chairs and lamps and the little stool in front of the scullery sink for the small boys to stand on.

Quaking with fear, Billy jumped into bed beside Graham. Graham reached over and patted his hand. "Don't be scared of him," he said. "He ain't so tough."

Billy gulped. "I don't like it when they call me names," he whimpered.

"Don't pay no attention," Graham said. "Everybody's got a nickname around here. Tony's nickname is Picker — you know why. And Tom is Pieface because he steals pies. And Benny is Benny-the-bulldog 'cause he looks like one."

"Tell him your nickname, why don'tcha," snorted Tony from across the room.

"You shut your gob!" Graham hissed.

"Stinker! Stinker!" taunted Tony.

"Grrrr!" growled Benny.

Then Tom said, "Ask him why his nickname's Stinker, why don'tcha."

"Why, Graham?" asked Bumper.

"Never you mind. Go to sleep."

* * *

The next night for supper Auntie Murna made a big pot of baked beans.

Graham loved baked beans but the baked beans didn't love him. No sooner had they gone sliding down his throat than his insides began to growl. And by the time he'd wiped his plate clean with a chunk of bread, he couldn't hold back the wind for another second.

All around the table the boys fanned the air and pinched their noses. So Graham fanned the air, too, and pinched his nose and glared down at Billy who was sitting, innocent as a lamb, beside him where Matthew used to sit. "Did you do that, Bumper?" he snapped.

Billy looked bewildered. "No–o–o," he said. "I thought you did."

"Well, for shame whoever did such a thing at the table," chided Mother Button as she clattered up their plates.

Then Flossie cut up one of Mr. Beetle's sponge cakes left over from the funeral and gave them each a thin slice on a plate.

Graham looked at the pale yellow colour of the cake and was reminded of Matthew's waxen face in the coffin. He pushed his slice over to Billy. "You can have it, Bump," he said, "if you promise not to do that at the table no more."

Flossie laughed and wagged her finger at Graham. Billy looked more puzzled than ever. But he took the cake and said, "Okay, I promise."

* * *

On Monday morning, Mother Button said to Graham, "I want you to take Billy Tree along with you and give him over to Miss Featherstone. She'll know what class he belongs in."

On the way to school Billy clung onto Graham's hand like a leech. "I'm scared of school, Stinker," he said.

Stopping short, Graham jerked Billy back by the arm. "You call me that one more time and I'll give you over to Picker and Pieface," he threatened, "or maybe even the Bulldog."

"But . . . but . . . everybody calls me Bumper. Nobody calls me Billy. So why can't I call you . . ."

"One more time," Graham warned.

"I–I–I forgot your real name already," sniffled Billy, wiping a drop off the end of his nose.

"It's Graham. Neill Graham Robbertson. That's Robbertson with two b's."

"Okay, Neill."

"Graham."

"Okay, Graham."

* * *

Miss Featherstone taught both the Fifth and Sixth classes, so Graham had counted himself lucky to be back in her class for another whole year. She let Billy sit with Graham for the whole morning. Then she took him to Mrs. Middleton's class of eight-year-olds.

Graham was happy just looking at Miss Featherstone. She was wearing a red dress and lipstick to match, and her black hair, instead of being swept up in a tight roll, was cut short and fluffy around her pretty face. "I hope she hasn't got wind of me running off again," Graham thought, "because I promised her I'd stay out of trouble, didn't I?"

Graham had made up his mind to work very hard this year, and not only to please his teacher. He had decided he wanted to be somebody when he grew up and Miss Featherstone had drilled into them that there was no substitute for hard work. You could be anything you wanted to be if you really tried, she had said.

"I'd like to be a London bus-driver," Graham daydreamed. He pictured himself in a busman's uniform behind the big black steering wheel of a red double-decker. "I wonder how much money is in their pay packet every week. A lot, I bet, because it's a hard job weaving that big bus in and out of all them cars and cabs."

Then something happened that spoiled his daydream.

Just before dismissal, a knock came at the classroom door. It was Mr. Prentice, the headmaster. He beckoned Miss Featherstone out into the hallway and shut the door. Through the window the class could see that the teacher and the headmaster were having a serious discussion.

When she came back in, Miss Featherstone's face was unusually stern and her fingers were laced together in front of her waist. "A grave matter has been brought to my attention," she said, her voice deadly serious. "Mrs. Middleton's handbag has disappeared from her desk. Mr. Prentice thinks it was stolen when she went outside during breaktime." Her eyes roamed all around the classroom, lighting on every face. "If anyone here knows anything about it, will you please come forward. No one will be allowed to leave the school until it is found."

Nobody said a word, so Miss Featherstone walked between the aisles questioning them one by one. Everybody shook their heads.

Graham hoped Bumper hadn't stolen it. No, Bumper was too timid. Scared of his own shadow.

Miss Featherstone gave them memory work to fill in the time. An hour passed in silence. At last Mr. Prentice came to the door again and said that they were dismissed.

Billy clung onto Graham's hand. "Somebody nicked my teacher's purse," he said, his voice wobbling nervously.

"I know," Graham said. Then he stopped and looked down into the little boy's worried green eyes.

"You didn't do it, did you, Bumper?" he asked.

"NO!" yelled Billy. "Did you?"

"'Course not," Graham snapped.

"Well, neither did I," cried Billy bumping into the corner postbox.

Tony Scooter ran past and gave Billy a thump on the head. Billy yelped and burst into tears.

Graham frowned down at him. "Stop blubbering, Bump," he said. "Picker won't let you alone as long as he can make you cry."

* * *

The next day, at breaktime, Graham went off by himself and sat under the giant horse-chestnut tree in the far corner of the schoolyard. The tree's branches spread out over his head like a huge umbrella. Crisp brown leaves covered the ground.

Graham was really missing Matthew. He had decided never to have a special mate again. "If you've got nobody, you can't lose nobody," he thought grimly.

Just then a big round chestnut the size of a plum, still in its prickly green shell, bonked him on the head and rolled to his feet. It reminded him of the story of Sir Isaac Newton who got bonked on the head by an apple and discovered gravity. He looked up into the tree and saw that the branches were loaded with ripe chestnuts just bursting to get out of their shells. "Perfect for playing conkers," he thought.

Shinnying up the tree, he stuffed his pockets full. He was just about to shinny back down when something brown and shiny caught his eye in the forked branch above his head. Reaching up he pulled down a brown leather handbag with the catch open. Snapping it shut, he slid to the ground.

Tony and Tom were standing under the tree. "Thief! Thief!" they bellowed as they raced towards the school.

"Hey!" Graham yelled after them, waving the purse in the air. "I didn't steal it. I found it!"

When Graham reached Miss Featherstone, she was listening to Tony and Tom. Then she listened to Graham. He told her exactly what happened.

"We'll have to take it to the headmaster and see what he has to say," she said.

"I found it in the horse-chestnut tree," he explained to Mr. Prentice. "I was collecting conkers and there it was, hid in the thick green leaves."

"What made you look for it there?" asked Mr. Prentice in an accusing voice.

"I wasn't looking for it, sir," Graham explained. "I was looking for conkers."

"Was anybody with you who can verify your story?" asked Mr. Prentice.

"No, sir, I was by myself. But it ain't a story. It's the truth. I found it by accident."

He felt the pressure of Miss Featherstone's fingers on his shoulder.

"The two boys that saw you with it say you knew exactly where to look," said Mr. Prentice.

"Well, they're liars!" shouted Graham, shrugging Miss Featherstone's hand away. "I found it by accident. I told you."

"Don't raise your voice to me, young man." The headmaster's bottom lip began to quiver, a sure sign that he was losing his temper. "Without a witness you don't have a leg to stand on." Then Graham heard him mutter as he walked away, "You Home boys are all alike: put you in a sack and throw you in the river and Lord knows who would come up first."

Chapter 18

The Magistrate

Graham couldn't understand why no one seemed to believe him. Mother Button said, "How can I trust a boy who runs off to London and comes home in a Black Maria?" Auntie Murna said, "I'm that disappointed in you, Graham. I always thought you were an honest boy." And Flossie said, "You're always getting yourself into scrapes, Graham. You cause more trouble than all the other boys put together."

Miss Featherstone said nothing. But he could tell by the furrow on her smooth white brow, and the way she avoided looking him in the eye, that she wasn't sure what to believe.

He didn't know what was going to happen to him. But he knew something was up because he caught Mother Button and Auntie Murna whispering in the kitchen and they hushed up the minute he came in. The smaller boys, all except Bumper, steered clear of him as if he had the plague. But the older boys, especially Tony and Tom, were enjoying every minute of his trouble.

On the third day after the incident he came home to find Flossie alone in the kitchen. She was walking back and forth balancing a pot on her head.

"Whatcha doing that for?" he asked, momentarily distracted.

"Mother told me to stop slouching or I'd end up bent over like Auntie Murna," Flossie said. Then she took the pot off her curly head and looked at him with sympathetic eyes. "She wants you in the sitting room," she said.

"Who wants me?" His heart began thumping.

"Mother, of course. She said the minute you got home to send you in. She's got something to tell you."

"What?" His heart sank to his boots.

"I can't tell you. Mother's got to tell you," she said.

Mother Button was sitting at the green baize card table she used when she had paperwork to do. On the table in front of her was a big brown envelope. Taking off her reading glasses, she beckoned him over.

"Graham," she said, tapping the envelope with her folded glasses. "There's a document in here concerning you."

"A document?" A wave of foreboding flowed over him like cold water. "What's it say?"

"It's a report concerning Mrs. Middleton's handbag," she said. "You are to appear in court and tell the magistrate your story."

"The magistrate? In court?"

"Yes. Next Tuesday at three o'clock. I'll take you there myself."

"But I didn't . . ."

"Don't say another word." She wagged the glasses in his face. "It's out of my hands entirely."

Graham had never been so frightened in his life. If the magistrate didn't believe him, like everybody else, then what would happen to him?

Time dragged like a lorry full of bricks until Tuesday. He avoided the other boys like the plague. He stayed outside, or in his bed, as much as possible. Then at last the awful day came.

Mother took him by the hand and marched him down Whiting Street, muttering all the way. Mr. Beetle and Widow Tweedy were standing on their doorsteps watching.

The courthouse was an ancient stone building. Inside was a wide hall with hardwood floors. Graham's feet began to drag as if there was lead in his boots. But Mother had his hand in a firm grip as she led him down the hall. They stopped in front of two huge oak doors. Above the double doors were the words "Juvenile Courtroom." A man in uniform pushed the doors open and they went in.

The courtroom had a high ceiling and arched windows. It was empty when he and Mother Button arrived. They sat in the front row on a long bench like a pew in a church. He could tell by the nervous wringing of her hands that Mother Button was very upset. The only thing she had said to him in the past week was that she didn't deserve to have such a troublesome boy in her charge. "I'm too old for it," she had complained. And when he had promised, hope-to-die, that he'd never ever run off again she just kept repeating, "It's out of my hands. It's out of my hands!"

Graham heard the heavy courtroom doors swing open again. Glancing furtively over his shoulder he saw

Mrs. Middleton and Miss Featherstone and Flossie Button coming down the aisle. Then, to his horror, right behind them came Tony Scooter, being prodded forward by a grim-faced Mr. Prentice.

Suddenly the chamber door at the front of the court-room swung open. A tall man in a black suit with silver hair, a Vandyke beard and horn-rimmed glasses entered the courtroom and strode towards the bench.

The court clerk stood at attention, facing the people. "All rise!" he commanded.

They rustled to their feet.

"Magistrate Horace Wickett presiding. You may be seated."

Mrs. Middleton was first to be called to the witness stand. Through tight lips she gave her testimony. She didn't actually accuse Graham, but her statement sounded like an accusation. "Yes," she said, pointing at Graham. "There sits the boy that found my handbag."

Mr. Prentice was next. Biting his lip to stop the quivering, he agreed with Mrs. Middleton.

The magistrate shuffled through some papers on his desk. Then he glanced up sharply. "Where is Anthony Scooter?" he asked.

Jumping up like a jack-in-the-box, his finger still buried in his nose, Tony shouted, "Here sir, me sir!"

"You may come forward . . . and remove that finger!"

Tony gave Graham a leery look as he made his way to the stand.

Something snapped inside Graham like a broken elastic band. Leaping to his feet he hollered, "HE'S GOING TO TELL ROTTEN LIES ABOUT ME!"

Banging his gavel, the magistrate yelled, "ORDER IN

THE COURT!" and Mother Button yanked Graham down by his coattail.

But all Tony said was, "I saw him . . ." he pointed at Graham, "shinnying down the tree with Mrs. Middleton's handbag."

Next it was Mother Button's turn. She didn't look at Graham. Instead she kept her eyes on the Magistrate. "I'm that disappointed in Graham Robbertson," she told him. "I thought he was a good boy, I really did. And I've done my best to be a mother to him. All my boys call me Mother." She pursed her lips and nodded her head. "I don't know if he stole the purse . . . it's hard for me to think such a thing . . . but . . ." she shook her head sadly . . . "he's caused me no end of trouble this past year."

"Trouble. What sort of trouble?" Magistrate Wickett leaned towards her.

"He runs off," she said.

"Runs off?" He raised his bushy eyebrows. "Where to?"

"To London. And to Ipswich. He stays out all night and worries me half to death. And I'm too old for such goings-on."

Taking off his horn-rimmed glasses the magistrate huffed on them and polished them with a white hanky. Then he said, "You may step down, Mrs. Button." Wrapping the arms of the glasses around his large ears, he peered over the rims. "Graham Robbertson," he said in a sonorous voice that filled the courtroom. "You may take the stand."

His legs wobbling like jelly, Graham managed to reach the witness box . . . "the prisoner's box," he thought. The courtroom clerk held out the Bible and he

104

placed his left hand on it. His right hand shook as he held it up.

"Do you swear to tell the truth, the whole truth and nothing but the truth so help you God?" asked the Clerk.

"I–I–I do," stammered Graham.

"LOUDER!" bawled the magistrate.

"I DO!" shouted Graham.

"Tell it then, what's your story?"

Graham took a deep breath. "It ain't a story," he insisted for the hundredth time. "It's the truth. I was gathering horse-chestnuts to play conkers . . . us boys always play conkers in the autumn . . . then I spied the handbag in the forked branch over my head. I didn't steal it. I found it."

"Was anyone with you to verify your story?"

There it was again, the word "story." Graham clamped his mouth shut and shook his head.

"Take your seat," said the judge, and Graham sat back down beside Mother Button.

All of a sudden, just when he thought that all was lost, Miss Featherstone jumped to her feet. "Your Honour," she addressed the bench in her clear, schoolteacher's voice.

"And who might you be, Madam?" frowned the judge.

"I am the boy's teacher." Miss Featherstone spoke with quiet dignity.

"You may come forward."

She came forward and took the oath.

"State your full name."

"Jennifer Featherstone."

"What a pretty name," Graham thought.

"You may proceed, Miss Featherstone."

"As I said, I am the boy's teacher." She glanced at Graham and for a split second their eyes met. Then she looked steadfastly towards the bench. "Graham Robbertson is a good pupil and I do not hesitate to vouch for his honesty. He has been in my home and has done garden work for me and his behaviour has been no less than honourable."

"That's right what the teacher says," piped up Flossie.

Judge Wickett stroked his beard and looked sternly at each person who had been in the witness box. Then his eyes, sharp as an owl's, swept back and forth between Graham and his teacher.

"You may step down, Miss Featherstone." She returned to her seat in the courtroom and the magistrate continued. "After hearing everyone's story, I am inclined to give the boy the benefit of the doubt." He took his glasses off and polished them again. "I played conkers, too, when I was a boy," he remarked quietly.

Mother Button squeezed Graham's hand.

"But . . . I think it is time, young man," he adjusted his glasses on his nose and stared straight at Graham with his black hawk-eyes, "that you had a change of environment. I am going to recommend that you be transferred from Mrs. Button's foster home in Bury St. Edmunds to Captain Flagg's Greystone School for Homeless Boys in Stony Stratford. There you will get the kind of training and discipline you so obviously need."

"But . . ." Graham had heard about Greystone School. Rumour had it that it was as tough as the army. And right now all he wanted to do was to go back home to Velma Villa. "But, but . . ."

"No buts about it." The magistrate banged his gavel.

"You can consider yourself lucky, because I was about to send you to Borstal (there was a collective gasp in the courtroom . . . everyone knew about Borstal). "But since your teacher has put in a good word for you, I am willing, with Mrs. Button's consent," he glanced at Mother Button, who bobbed her head vigorously, "to give you another chance. Captain Flagg has a fine reputation of making boys into men. Therefore, you will be removed to Greystone at the beginning of next week." Banging the gavel once more he shouted, "Case dismissed!" and swept out of the courtroom.

A man? Graham felt himself shrinking in his boots. He was just a boy. He felt tears stinging behind his eyes; he held them back with all his might because he didn't want Tony Scooter to see him crying.

* * *

The night before Graham was to leave Velma Villa he couldn't sleep. He hadn't been able to eat a bite even though Auntie Murna had made his two favourite foods for his last supper: Bubble and Squeak (potatoes and cabbage fried into crispy patties) and Spotted Dick (boiled suet pudding stuffed with plump sultanas). His empty stomach was rumbling ominously so he got up and went to the bathroom and drank two glasses of water. The water filled the void and he went back to bed.

Across the room Tom spoke in a loud whisper, "I heard they cane the boys every Saturday night at Greystone."

Then Benny-the-bulldog growled, "Yah, and I heard they have pig's head for dinner every Sunday."

Pop went Tony's finger. "And I heard the new boys have to eat the pig's eyes!" he snorted.

"Well, I heard the nose-pickers get the snout," Graham shot back.

"Is that right, Stink . . . I mean Graham?" asked Billy Tree.

"How should I know," Graham snapped "I never been there. And neither have Picker nor Pieface nor Bulldog. So go to sleep."

Billy pulled his knees up to his chest, bumping Graham on the back. "I don't want you to go, Gray," he whispered. "I'll be scared when you're gone."

Graham turned towards Billy and whispered in his ear, "Well, remember what I told you, Bump. If you cry they'll torment you all the more. So stop right now. You got to learn to be tough. I was scared, too, when I first came to Velma Villa. And look at me now."

"Okay," Billy gulped. "I'll try to be just like you, Stink— I mean Gray."

"What you two whispering about?" asked Tom, bobbing up in his bed.

"None of your business," snapped Graham.

Tom grunted and flopped back down.

"See what I mean," whispered Graham. "Bullies ain't nothing but cowards in disguise."

Billy sighed. "I'll miss you Gray," he said.

"I'll miss you, too, Billy."

He put his arm around the little boy, who went to sleep comforted. But Graham lay awake all night planning ways to escape from Captain Flagg's school.

Chapter 19

Greystone

GREYSTONE SCHOOL FOR HOMELESS BOYS. The big scrolly letters across the black iron gates made Graham feel more of an orphan than he had ever felt before.

Mother Button pushed open the heavy gates and they walked up the flagged path to the huge grey stone building. Two wide steps flanked the heavy arched doorway.

Standing on the top step, Mother Button said, "Ring the bell, Graham." He didn't budge so she reached up and pushed the button herself.

The door was opened almost instantly by the biggest man Graham had ever seen. His body filled the doorway, towering over him and Mother Button.

"Welcome to Greystone," he boomed. "I am Captain Flagg. You may follow me." He led the way down a long hall into an office and motioned them to sit on two brown leather armchairs in front of a massive desk. Then he sat behind the desk on a swivel chair. He was an imposing man with thick black hair, a thick black moustache, and steel grey eyes.

There were papers for Mother Button to sign, and Graham had to sign them, too. He could hardly see through the blur of tears so he just signed on the dotted line where Mother pointed.

Glancing at the signatures, the Captain remarked, "Robbertson with two b's. Are you sure?" The steel grey eyes seemed to bore into Graham like a drill.

Graham swallowed the lump in his throat and managed to say, "It's spelt that way on my birth certificate. So it must be right, mustn't it?" then he added, "Sir."

"Humph!" grunted the Captain, then he slid the signed papers into a large brown envelope. "How old are you, Robbertson?" His voice rumbled like thunder.

"I'm twelve, sir," answered Graham.

"Then we'll try you in Mister Bolton's class. Mr. Bolton is hard on rules. And so am I. Greystone's Rules are as follows:" He held up his left hand and began counting on his fingers: "No running in the halls, no swearing, no shouting, and no bullying and no talking after lights out." He reversed to his right hand. "Your daily chores are as follows: making your bed, cleaning the washbasin, and taking your turn stoking the boiler and scrubbing the halls. If you behave yourself and follow these rules you should do well here at Greystone. Do I make myself clear, Robbertson?"

"Y–y–yes, sir."

"Then you may say goodbye to your foster mother."

The Captain waited as Graham walked with Mother Button down the long hall to the front doors. Turning towards him, she licked the palm of her hand and smoothed down the tuft of his hair. "Now promise me,

Graham, that you'll be a good boy and make me proud," she said. He knew he couldn't make such a promise so he just said, "I'll be fine, Mother. Don't worry."

Then the Captain's loud voice interrupted, "Come along, young man, look sharp. Goodbye, madam."

Lugging the suitcase with all his worldly goods inside, Graham struggled after the Captain up a wide staircase and down a long hall to a door with a sign on it which read "Dormitory 1". The Captain pushed open the door and they entered a long narrow room with many iron bedsteads lined up against opposite walls. Above each bed was a number from 1 to 22. Every bed had a grey wool blanket tucked as tight as a drum under a flat mattress. At the head of each bed was a blue-striped pillow.

Pointing to bed number 2, the Captain said, "This is where you'll sleep. Stow your case under the bed and come along with me. I'll show you to your classroom."

Back down the stairs they went, past the office, to the end of the hall. Another corridor led off to the right. "The classrooms are in the east wing," explained the Captain. Then he knocked sharply on the end door.

"Mister Bolton," the Captain said to the man who answered his knock. "This is Graham Robbertson, our new boy. That's Robbertson with two b's." He looked down at Graham. "In you go, young man, and do your best." He gave Graham a thump on the back and left.

Mister Bolton was the exact opposite of Captain Flagg. He was a skinny little man in a pin-striped suit and a red bow tie. And there was something funny about his ginger-coloured hair. It looked like a bird's nest sitting crooked on his head.

Graham felt himself the target of dozens of curious eyes.

"This is our new boy, Graham Robbertson, with two b's," a sarcastic little sniff escaped the teacher's pointed nose. "You may take a seat, Robbertson." Snapping his fingers like a pair of scissors, he pointed to an empty desk in the middle of the room.

Legs shot out from either side as Graham made his way down the aisle, and he stumbled over them.

Chapter 20

Initiation

He didn't speak to anybody that first day. He just followed the crowd and got bumped and jostled down the halls. He sighed with relief when nighttime came and he could take refuge in his narrow dormitory bed.

That night his roommates had a right ding-dong pillow fight. Knocking each other over the head they leapt from bed to bed. They even bounced off the end of Graham's bed, but they didn't include him in their fun and he was glad to be left alone.

Then Captain Flagg appeared at the dormitory door and shouted, "Lights out! Good night, boys!"

"Good night, sir!" they chorused.

As suddenly as the lights switched off, the rough-and-tumble stopped.

"I'll never get used to this place," Graham worried. He felt a lump the size of a plum rise up in his throat. He swallowed hard and hugged his knees to his chest. A wave of homesickness washed over him and he felt as if he was going to drown.

"How am I ever gonna get out of here?" he thought hopelessly. "It's gonna be a lot harder than escaping from Velma Villa."

At last he escaped into a troubled sleep. He dreamed, as he often did, about his mother. But in this dream she was more elusive than ever, always disappearing around corners.

* * *

The first week at Greystone was a nightmare for Graham. Every day he got jostled and knocked about in the halls. Then every night the boys initiated him with mean tricks.

The first trick they played on him was to stretch a string between his bed and the next one, which sent him sprawling. He bumped his head on the floor, but his pride was hurt a lot worse than his head.

The next night they sprinkled pepper between his sheets. His skin itched and burned for days but he didn't dare complain.

Another night he woke to the sound of moaning and chains rattling overhead. That trick didn't fool him for a second, because he had played it himself at Bury St. Edmunds. Whenever a new boy arrived at Velma Villa, Picker or Pieface or Benny-the-bulldog would sneak up into the attic and moan and groan and drag a dog chain across the boards. Then they'd tell the terrified new-comer — usually a little boy like Billy Tree — that it was Garfield the ghost who had hung himself in the attic three hundred years ago.

The worst trick at Greystone was the cheese. Malcolm Dray, the head boy of the dormitory, came in one night carrying a plate of crackers and cheese. Light yellow cheese, it was, cut up into bite-size pieces. Malcolm offered the treat to several boys and they all took a piece and held it between their fingers, grinning from ear to ear. Then he came over to where Graham was sitting on the edge of his bed. "Help yourself," he said in a deceptively friendly voice.

Graham didn't stop to wonder at Malcolm's sudden friendliness.

"Thanks!" he said. Choosing the biggest piece, he popped it into his mouth and began chomping.

"AAAGGHH!" Gagging and spluttering he spat it out onto the floor. Yellow foam oozed out between his teeth and bubbled down his chin. SOAP! The awful tasting cheese was carbolic soap!

Racing to the bathroom, he held his mouth under the tap and rinsed and gagged for fifteen minutes. When he came back to the dorm the boys were all falling down laughing. Graham balled up his fists and glared at them furiously. But he knew he was out-numbered by far, so he slunk into bed, tears of shame stinging his eyeballs.

In spite of all the nighttime shenanigans no one had really talked to him, except the head boy, Malcolm Dray, who barked out orders every morning: make your beds, clean your basins, polish your boots, scrub the floors, wash the dishes. It made Velma Villa seem like a holiday resort by comparison. Graham decided to write to Mother Button and beg her to take him back.

He managed to sneak a piece of paper and a stub of pencil into the bathroom. Kneeling on the floor he used the toilet seat cover for a desk. "Dear Mother," he scribbled. "I don't like it here. If I promise in writing never to run off again and . . ."

Suddenly a loud banging rattled the door.

"Whoever's in there —" Graham recognized Malcolm's voice. "— you've got ten seconds to come out. One Picadilly . . . two Picadilly . . . three Picadilly . . ." Graham flushed the paper down the toilet and jumped out the door on the count of nine Picadilly.

Every night when the games were over and the lights went out, and just before he fell asleep, Graham would plan his escape. The planning brought him comfort. But there was one thing that stopped him in his tracks: Captain Flagg's cane. It was more menacing by far than Mother Button's wooden spoon.

Chapter 21

Sunday at Greystone

Graham hated Greystone — except on Sundays. The boys had no jobs to do on Sundays. After a delicious breakfast of rashers and scrambled eggs, they changed into their church clothes: short black trousers, black socks, black boots, white collars and black bow ties. Then off they marched to chapel like a line of trained penguins following after Captain and Mrs. Flagg.

Graham could never keep his mind on the sermon, thinking about the Sunday dinner that was to come right after church. He used to think that Auntie Murna's Sunday dinners were the best. But not compared to Mrs. Mulligan's Sunday feasts: thick slices of roast beef and Yorkshire pudding with a well of brown gravy in the middle. Snowy mashed potatoes and broad beans and diced carrots glistening with real dairy butter. Sometimes they had crackling roast pork (not pig's head as Picker had predicted) with apple sauce and pan-browned potatoes. And for dessert . . . oh, Mrs. Mulligan was champion at dessert . . . chocolate cream pie or lemon meringue tarts or taffy sticky-buns all washed down with milky tea. Never vegetable water!

But even the Sunday feasts were not enough to make Graham happy at Greystone. He missed the freedom of attending the local school in Bury St. Edmunds. Here at Greystone you ate and slept and went to school all in the same building. And you could never leave the premises without permission. He wondered if red-haired Colleen missed him a little bit. And Miss Featherstone, did she ever think of him?

On the Monday of the third week, as he was being swept down the hall like a leaf in a tidal wave, a boy Graham had never seen before broke from the pack and came up beside him.

"Hello! My name's Andrew Noble-Gresty," he yelled above the hubbub. "It's got a hyphen."

"Hello, yourself. My name's Graham Robbertson," Graham yelled back. "It's got two b's."

Andrew Noble-Gresty was a tall lanky boy like Matthew. But there the resemblance ended. Andrew had ruddy cheeks and huge brown eyes and black curly hair that tumbled over his forehead.

"Where'd you come from, Gray?" he asked as they swarmed like bees into the dining hall.

"Bury St. Edmunds." Graham had to yell above the clamour of voices and scraping chairs on the bare wood floor.

"Never heard of it," Andrew yelled back as they sat down side by side.

"I been here two weeks. How come I've never seen you before?" Graham hollered.

"I been in the Infirmary. I got a gumboil lanced and

it went rancid and made me sick." He opened his mouth and showed Graham the gooey red hole.

Just then Captain Flagg, standing behind the head table, rang the dinner bell and the dining hall fell instantly silent.

Graham kept his eyes on his plate. But the silence lasted so long that he looked up to see what was happening. The Captain's steely grey eyes were staring straight at him. "Our new boy, Graham Robbertson, has been with us for two weeks now. So I think it's time he took his turn. Robbertson, will you please stand up and say grace?"

Graham froze in his seat. Grace? That was one thing he could not do, speak in public, but he was too stubborn to admit it. A minute ticked by and Graham remained frozen to his seat. Finally Andrew poked him in the ribs. "He means you!" he hissed.

Struggling to his feet, his heart in his mouth, Graham stammered, "N–n–no, sir, I c–c–can't, sir," and sat down.

Dead silence fell. The only sound that could be heard in the vast dining hall was the ticking of the pendulum clock on the wall.

Then the Captain broke the silence. "Very well, Robbertson, you are excused. Go to my office and wait for me there."

It was the longest walk of his life: from his seat at the table to the dining-hall door and down the long corridor to the Captain's office.

He sat on the chair where he had sat that first day with Mother Button beside him and let his eyes roam around the room. Framed pictures of classrooms of boys from other years hung on the dark wood panelled walls.

Under each picture was a date, beginning in 1921, all the way up to 1945. On a big blotter on the Captain's desk lay a pad of stationery. Graham could read the heading upside-down. "Captain Theodore Flagg, Headmaster. Greystone School for Homeless Boys."

The world "homeless" made him acutely aware of being an orphan. He hadn't felt so much like an orphan at Mother Button's because Velma Villa was a house, a regular big house that sat on a sidewalk on Whiting Street. Greystone, with its halls and towers and pillars and turrets, was more like an institution.

His empty stomach began to rumble. He broke wind,

then jumped up and fanned the seat of the chair. He wiped the fringe of his hair back from his sweaty forehead nervously.

When, at last, he heard the Captain's heavy footsteps in the hallway he dropped his eyes to the carpet.

Closing the big oak door of his office, Captain Flagg went behind his desk and swung into his swivel chair. He waited, not saying a word, until Graham finally raised his head.

"Well. What have you got to say for yourself, Robbertson?" growled the headmaster.

"I–I–I'm sorry, sir," was all Graham could think of to say.

"That's not good enough, Robbertson." The Captain leaned across his desk, his fingers laced together, his piercing eyes boring into Graham's. "What made you say no? You'll sit there till you tell me so you might as well own up."

"Well, sir," Graham said, "Mother Button always said I must have inherited it from my mother or father."

"Inherited what?"

"My stubborn streak, sir."

"And did you?"

"I don't know, sir. You see I never met them . . . my mother or father. But Mother Button says I'm the stubbornest boy she ever met so it must be in my blood. So you see, sir, it's not really my fault. I can't help it."

Graham thought he saw Captain Flagg's lips flicker. Not quiver with anger like Mr. Prentice's, but flicker like Miss Featherstone's when she was trying to hide a smile. The Captain combed his black moustache with his fingers and when he took his hand away his bottom lip was a firm line. "Well, that excuse won't work here at Greystone." He swivelled out of his chair and came around the desk to sit on the corner, one long leg swinging, back and forth, past Graham's knees. "I'm going to let you off this time, Robbertson, but don't ever let me hear the word "no" come out of your mouth again. Understood?"

"No, sir . . . I mean yes, sir." Leaping up, Graham saluted the Captain because he couldn't think what else to do. Then he bolted for the door.

"Robbertson! I haven't dismissed you yet."

Graham stopped in his tracks, his gizzards grumbling.

"You may go to the kitchen and tell cook — Mrs. Mulligan — that I said to give you a bite to eat. Then straight to bed. Understand?"

"Yes, sir. Thank you, sir."

"Yes, Captain Flagg. That's Flagg with two g's."

"Yes, Captain Flagg."

"Dismissed!"

* * *

That night his roommates suddenly took an interest in him. As soon as they were all back in the dormitory they began firing questions. "What happened in the office?" "Did you get a caning?" "How many whacks did he give you?" "Did you get a detention?" "What did he say?"

"Who?" teased Graham.

Andrew threw a shoe in his direction and Graham ducked just in time, so the shoe hit the wall. "You know who," he cried. "Flagg the Windbag."

"He said I can't say 'No' no more," laughed Graham.

"Is that all? You lucky dog."

A pillow came flying through the air and hit him on

the head. He grabbed his own pillow and whacked the boy nearest him. And that was the start of his first big ding-dong pillow fight.

When the lights went out and they all settled down Graham knew he had been accepted. He was one of the boys at last.

Chapter 22

Homesick

1st December, 1946

Dear Miss Featherstone,

*   I'm fitting in pretty good here at Greystone School. I'm glad you made me work so hard last year because I am ahead of some of the boys in my class. My teacher is Mister Bolton. His first name is Bertram. The boys call him "Perty Bertie" because he smells like perfume and he wears bow ties and a red wig that sits crooked on his head. And they call Captain Flagg "Flagg the Windbag" because he talks a lot. And loud! I guess it's normal to call your teachers funny nicknames behind their backs. But I did not call you names behind your back, Miss Featherstone, because I like you too much.*

*   I have been here three weeks and so far I have not got a caning. The second week I said "No" when I should have said "Yes" and I got a telling-off by Captain Flagg and sent to bed early. But that's all. So that's not too bad, is it?*

*   I made a new friend here whose name is Andrew Noble-Gresty. But I don't want to get too matey with him in case*

*he dies like Matthew did. I still miss Matty. I have decided
to be a loner all my life. Unless, of course, I meet a nice
lady like you when I grow up, and get married. That
would be different.*

> *I am very truly yours, Miss Featherstone.*
> *I mean that sincerely.*
> *Neill Graham Robbertson.*

Next Graham wrote a long letter to Mother Button
and Auntie Murna and Flossie. At the end of Mother's
letter he added: "P.S. Could I please come home for
Christmas?" And he also enclosed a note for Billy Tree.

In a week he had letters back from all but Flossie.
Mother said that Flossie was too flustered to write
because she had just got herself engaged.

> *You remember that nice young man that took Flossie to
> the Picture House on Saturday nights? His name is Adam
> Hook and he has a Fruit Shop in town. Well, he asked me
> for Flossie's hand, and since her father is no longer with
> us, God rest his soul, I said yes because he comes from a
> good family. The only problem is his name: Adam Hook.
> Flossie says she wants to keep her own name in the middle,
> and Auntie Murna said, "That will sound foolish: Flossie
> Button-Hook." But Flossie just laughed and said she
> didn't care so I said to Murna, "Well, that's her own
> lookout, isn't it?*
>
> *I'm glad to hear you are settling in at your new school,
> Graham, and proving what we've always said about you
> here at Velma Villa, that you are a good boy. So try not to
> get into trouble. And don't run off anymore.*
>
> *Today being the first week of December, there was frost*

126

on the windowpane and ice on the pavement. I had to sprinkle it with salt so the postman wouldn't take a fall. Then I sent Tony out to get the box of Christmas decorations from the shelter.

Graham felt a pang of jealousy so strong it hurt his throat.

I am busy knitting all the boys khaki socks and mittens with the yarn I had left over from the war. So what with Christmas baking to do and Flossie's wedding cake to make (she and Adam have set the date for January 18) I will be too busy to write until later in the New Year. But you'll always be in my thoughts and prayers, Graham, rest assured.

> *With love from your foster mother*
> *and Auntie Murna*
> *and Flossie soon to be Button-Hook.*

P.S. I'm sorry to say we can't have you home for Christmas, Graham, because Billy Tree and our new boy, Timmy Little, have come down with the German measles and the house is under quarantine. Just last week I caught the two of them pouring their lovely orange carrot juice down the kitchen drain. So no wonder they got sick, wasting vitamins like that! Here's Flossie to add a word after all.

Flossie's handwriting swirled merrily across the bottom of the page.

Happy Christmas, Graham! From your foster sister Flo. Please note the new spelling of my name. Adam, my fiancé, says Flossie is a cow's name so he calls me Flo. Isn't that lovely?

Also enclosed in Mother's letter was a postal order for one pound, sixpence, with a note paperclipped to it that read: "From all of us here at Velma Villa, Merry Christmas."

And a scribbly note from Billy Tree.

"Dear Gray," wrote Billy,

I was glad to get yur letter. My teacher had a tock with Tony and Tom and now they just call me names but don't hit me. But I am much braver now becus I have Timmy Litle to look out for. He is the new boy who came just after you left. The only trubbel is he waters the bed most every night so I promised him tuppence (my auntie sent it to me) if he stops and he hasn't done it for two nights now. Guess what Tony and Tom nicknamed him? Piddle-Widdle! Timmy and me have got the measles and Mother painted us pink with calamine lotion. I am not very sick but Timmy is. He has got red spots all over him, even on his bum. I hope you don't get sick from the germs on this paper, Gray. Goodbye for now. Have you got a nickname in the new school? I sure hope it's a diffrunt one.

Your troo frend, Billy Tree.

P.S. I am doing good in school except for speling.

Waves of homesickness washed over Graham as he read the letters. He'd even be glad to see Picker and Pieface. And Christmas had always been a happy time at Velma Villa. There had been presents under the tree for each boy: homemade knitted things and a small gift such as a pencil sharpener or a game of Snakes and Ladders. For Christmas dinner Auntie Murna always roasted two fat hens, because Mother didn't like goose, and they had plenty of vegetables. On Christmas Day, instead of vegetable water in their mugs, the boys were always treated to foamy hot cocoa!

Christmas at Greystone

Although they were all homeless boys at Greystone, still some had relatives who sent them presents in the post.

Graham and Andy were among the boys who were truly orphans. Andy's parents had been killed in the war. His father had been home on leave from the Army when a Messerschmitt crashed into their house and killed them both, along with the German pilot. Luckily for Andy, he had been at school. He had no relatives to live with, so he was sent to Greystone. Christmas was not a happy time for Graham and Andrew.

After breakfast on Christmas Day, Captain and Mrs. Flagg handed out the pile of presents from under the sparkling tree. As their names were called the boys stepped forward, one by one. Each boy received a bag of sweets and a present wrapped in red tissue paper. You could tell it was a book right through the paper.

When the books were all given out, the special gifts that had come in the mail were collected by the lucky few; these were all wrapped in special Christmas paper.

Graham and Andrew were sitting at the back of the room near the door. "Let's get outta here, Andy!" Graham whispered. They slipped out quietly without being seen. Then they ran upstairs to the dormitory and sat side by side against the top rail of Graham's bed. Sucking on sweets, they tore open their presents. Andrew's book was *Treasure Island* by Robert Louis Stevenson. Graham's was *The Call of the Wild* by Jack London.

"That's a good story you've got there," Graham told Andy. "I read it to my mate once."

"Why'd you have to read it to him? Can't he read?"

"He can't read no more because he's dead. But it was him got me interested in books because when he was very sick, before he died, he was too tired to read to himself and I had to read to him. Matthew was very smart, and when I made a mistake he made me say it over, and now one of my favourite things to do is read." He opened his new book and on the fly-leaf was written, in Captain Flagg's bold black handwriting, "To Graham Robbertson, Merry Christmas from Greystone School, 1946."

Just then the dormitory door swung open and there was Captain Flagg himself, his big frame filling the doorway.

"What are you two boys doing up here all by yourselves on Christmas Day?" he asked in his booming voice.

"Well, sir," answered Graham, "it's no fun for Andy and me, watching the other boys opening their special presents from their families."

Captain Flagg furrowed his brow and stroked his chin. "Well, never you mind, lads," he said. "Someday it will all be made up to you. Mark my words! Merry Christmas!"

"Merry Christmas, Captain," they chorused as Captain Flagg turned on his heel and left.

"Why is he called Captain, I wonder?" said Graham.

"Because he's a war hero," explained Andrew. "He gets to keep the title Captain for life, and King George even pinned a medal on him."

"What for?"

"Well, he was in a German prison camp for three years and he helped lots of his men escape. If he'd got caught he'd have been shot by a firing squad."

"Cor! That sure makes him a hero." Graham closed his book with a smack. "Let's go outside. I think I hear a snowball fight."

* * *

That night in his bed, Graham heard Captain Flagg's words echoing in his head. "Never you mind, lads, someday it will all be made up to you. Mark my words!" He wasn't sure why, but the Captain's words made him feel much better.

And he had enjoyed the Christmas dinner of roast goose (it took six big geese to feed the lot of them — the biggest birds he'd ever seen) and golden-brown roast potatoes and orange carrot sticks and bright green Brussels sprouts all glistening with goosey-brown gravy. And for dessert, plum pudding that Captain Flagg set alight with a long wooden match. Blue flames shot up and seemed to consume the pudding, then, with a sudden pouf! the fire went out. Then Mrs. Flagg served up the rich brown pudding in glass dessert dishes and drowned it in creamy custard sauce.

The pudding was delicious, but Graham had been disappointed that there were no thruppence or silver sixpences hidden in it like there used to be at Velma Villa.

New Year's

For Graham and Andrew, New Year's was a lot more fun than Christmas. On New Year's Eve all the boys ran out into the street armed with pots and pans and clackers and horns and whistles.

Mrs. Mulligan gave Graham and Andrew each a saucepan and a wooden spoon. "Now don't you put a dent in them, mind!" she called after them as they ran out onto the snowy street with their homemade noise-makers.

At the stroke of midnight cathedral bells rang out gloriously in the still cold air. Yipping and yapping like a bunch of puppies let out of a pen, the boys banged their pots and pans and blew their horns and whistles with all their might.

Shouts of "Happy New Year!" could be heard from all over the town of Stony Stratford. It was 1947 and the war was, at last, falling into the past. The future looked peaceful and bright.

After the celebration, their cheeks shining like red

apples, the boys tumbled back into the warmth of the fire-lit school. Then they swarmed like bees down the wide corridor to the dining hall for Greystone's annual New Year's treat: steaming hot cocoa and mouth-watering mincemeat pies.

* * *

By the time they got into their nightshirts they were all too excited to settle down to sleep.

"Who's up for Truth, Dare or Promise?" said Malcolm Dray in a loud whisper.

"Never heard of it," Graham said. "How do you play?"

"Easy," explained Malcolm. "After lights-out and the staff is sound asleep, I'll dare you to go knock on the Captain's door."

"Captain Flagg?"

"O'course. We only got one Captain." Malcolm laughed. "And you can't cheat because another boy has got to follow you down to make sure you tell the truth and keep your promise."

"I'll follow him!" volunteered Andrew.

So they jumped into their beds and when they heard Captain Flagg's big boots echoing down the hall they snuggled under their blankets as innocent as lambs and wished him a sleepy Happy New Year as he flicked out the lights.

The dormitory was so dark and quiet you could have heard a feather fall. Graham almost fell asleep waiting. Then suddenly a torch as bright as the full moon was beamed into his face.

"C'mon!" Malcolm yanked his blanket off. "You ain't going to get out of it."

"Never said I wanted to," yawned Graham, rubbing

his eyes. "You coming, Andy?"

"I'm right behind you, Gray."

Shivering from the chilly draft, as the old school's windows rattled in the winter wind, the boys crept on bare feet the length of the hall and down the cold hardwood stairs.

Captain Flagg was the only staff member who had a private flat in the school, not only because he was headmaster, but because he was a war hero.

"Which door is his?" Graham whispered to Andrew.

"First one past the dining hall."

"Left or right?"

"Left."

The hall's carpeted runner muffled their footsteps and they reached the door without making a sound.

Standing in front of the big oak door, Graham was seized by sudden panic. He hesitated so long that Andrew whispered. "You got to do it, you know."

"I know," hissed Graham. Steeling himself he made a fist and gave three sharp raps with his knuckles.

"Run!" cried Andy and he shot down the hall like an arrow with Graham hot on his heels.

Halfway down the runner Graham tripped over something soft and went flying head-over-heels. "Meow!" yowled Kipper the cat and the hall light flashed on like a bolt of lightning.

Flat on his back on the carpet, Graham stared up into the steely grey eyes of Captain Flagg.

"On your feet, Robbertson!" bellowed the Captain.

Graham leapt up, shaking from head to toe.

"Who put you up to this trick, Robbertson?" demanded the headmaster.

136

"N–no one, sir," Graham stammered.

The Captain grabbed him by his nightshirt. "It's an old trick that you didn't think up yourself. So who's the ringleader? Tell me or it's the cane for you tomorrow."

"Oh, now, Theodore." Mrs. Flagg stood at the door to their flat, shaking her head. A curler popped out of her salt-and-pepper hair and rolled across the floor. Kipper pounced on it as if it were a mouse. "It's the lad's first New Year's. You don't want him to remember it with a caning, now do you? I'm sure he'll never do it again. Isn't that right, boy?"

"Yes, Mrs. Flagg," agreed Graham.

Captain Flagg let go of Graham's shirt. "Well, I've had enough of being wakened in the middle of the night." He crossed his arms and glared down at Graham. "But if he confesses who the ringleader is I'll excuse him this time. Well, Robbertson?"

"I–I–I can't tell you, sir," stammered Graham.

"Then you will report to my office first thing in the morning." He snapped off the hall light and Graham heard Mrs. Flagg muttering, "Tsk, tsk, tsk!" as she picked up the cat and followed her husband into their flat.

Feeling his way along the cold painted wall of the dark hall, Graham reached the stairs and sprinted the rest of the way back to the dormitory.

Muffled snickers and snorts rippled from one end of the long room to the other.

Crawling under his wool blanket, Graham hunched his knees up under his nightshirt and squeezed his cold toes between his fingers.

"Gray," Andrew whispered from the next bed. "I'm sorry I let you down, mate."

"You ain't my mate," Graham snapped in a disgusted whisper. "I got no mate. 'Specially one that leaves me in the lurch."

"I said I'm sorry," muttered Andrew.

"You two shut your gobs!" barked Malcolm from across the room.

It took Graham hours to get to sleep that night. When at last he did, he dreamed he was in London. It was springtime and he was strolling along the Embankment picking yellow daffodils. Just then he saw the hem of his mother's skirt disappearing around a corner. But when he ran to the corner she had vanished. He looked down at the daffodils. They were all dead and drooping in his hand

* * *

For the second time he found himself in the hot seat. Captain Flagg kept him waiting on tenterhooks. Then he entered the office and glared down at Graham until Graham finally looked up. Their eyes met and for a long time the headmaster didn't speak.

Then he said, "That makes twice. Three times and you're out. Dismissed!"

Graham could hardly believe his luck. The boys had been making bets on how many whacks of the cane he'd get. And for some strange reason he'd got off scot-free.

That night in bed he pondered the Captain's words. "That makes twice. Three times and you're out."

Then, like a light switching on in his head, Graham suddenly understood. "Out" meant Borstal, the dreaded Remand Home.

Fear clutched his heart like a fist.

Chores

The threat of Borstal, which conjured up a jail full of bullies, helped Graham decide to turn over a new leaf. He would work hard at his lessons and try to keep out of trouble. No more pranks, or cheeky answers popping out of his mouth. He would learn to keep his lips sealed and his temper under control. He remembered Mother Button saying that the New Year was like a clean sheet of paper — there were no mistakes on it. He vowed to use the brand new start.

Graham worked harder than he'd ever done in his life. He paid strict attention in class and studied his lessons at night. Still, he kept his quest for his mother in the back of his mind. Sometimes there were school trips to London and to Cambridge and to other places. He would keep a sharp eye out and look for her then.

In the meantime, he did his daily chores with a will and saved his earnings. All the boys at Greystone had chores to do and they got paid according to their squad. When the Easter exams were over, Graham found he had

Stoking the boiler.

achieved his highest marks ever. Captain Flagg rewarded him by moving him up to Fifth Squad: sixpence a week.

Greystone School was surrounded by lawns and trees and flowers, much like a gentleman's estate. With the coming of spring, there were lots of outdoor chores to do.

One sunny day in late April, Captain Flagg called the Fifth Squad together and hand-picked six boys for a special job. Graham was one of them.

"Follow me!" Captain Flagg boomed, and he led them out onto the grounds carrying a canvas bag. Inside the bag were six pairs of scissors. Handing each boy a pair he said, with an unmistakable twinkle in his eye, "Now lads, we're expecting a visitor today. His name is Inspector Townsend and he is being sent from Head Office. He'll be here . . ." He checked his pocket-watch. ". . . in exactly fifteen minutes. So spread out along the walkway and start trimming as if your life depended on it."

"But, sir? Why don't we use . . ."

"No questions. Just follow orders, and you'll see."

So the boys got down on their hands and knees on either side of the flagstone walk and started clipping.

The inspector arrived right on the dot. The Captain met him at the iron gates and led him down the garden path.

Halfway down the Inspector stopped, looked around and scratched his head. "Why are your boys cutting the grass with scissors?" he asked curiously.

"Well, sir, our lawnmower is old and broken beyond repair. I put in a request for a new one from Head Office and was turned down unequivocally. So we're doing the best we can with what we've got. It might take a week to finish the job, but we'll do it, won't we lads?"

"YES SIR!" they chorused.

Two days later a brand new lawnmower was delivered to Greystone School and the boys all earned an extra sixpence.

Another job that Graham's squad was assigned to do was rake the grounds behind the school for a hockey pitch. That's when Graham found out how Stony Stratford got its name. The squad filled hundreds of buckets of stones before the field was smooth enough to play on.

* * *

Graham was gaining confidence and feeling happy and at home at Greystone. He had lots of friends and no enemies, and he had finally stopped mooning about Velma Villa.

One night, a lump under his mattress was making him uncomfortable and keeping him awake. He slipped his hand between the mattress and the springs and his fingers found his moneybag. He realized with a jolt that he had stopped planning his getaway. And he had almost forgotten the picture of his mother that he had carried in his mind all these years. Poking the bag back under the mattress, he sighed and fell into a troubled sleep.

The next day Captain Flagg spoke to him in the hallway just outside the classroom. "Robbertson," he said in his no-nonsense voice. "Since you have been showing promise in mathematics, I am transferring you to Mr. Bugle's class. I feel you will benefit from the expertise of our Maths specialist."

The news gave Graham a sinking feeling in his stomach. He didn't like the idea of changing classes. Now that he was working hard at his lessons, he had been getting along just fine with Mr. Bolton. And "Barney Google," as the boys had dubbed Mr. Bugle because of his big googly eyes behind thick, round glasses, had a reputation for being a bully who picked on new boys.

Sure enough, the teacher snapped at him on the very first day. "Robbertson! What's that you've got in your mouth?"

Forgetting his vow not to be cheeky, Graham said, "My tongue, sir."

Snorts and snickers rippled over the classroom.

"That's not funny, Robbertson. What else have you got in there?" He leaned over Graham's desk and raised his chin with the tip of his ruler. "Open wide!" he commanded.

His classmate's snickers made Graham even more nervy. Darting his tongue out like a snake, he curled it up until it touched the tip of his nose.

Crack! The steel-edged ruler slashed across Graham's knuckles. Blood spurted out and dripped on his exercise book. Tears stung his eyes but he gritted his teeth and didn't cry out.

At last the twelve o'clock dinner bell rang.

"Class dismissed!" shouted the teacher.

Instead of going to the dining hall, Graham made straight for the front door. Andrew followed him and they sat on the flagstone steps. It was a balmy spring day and yellow daffodils were blooming in the flower beds.

"Does it hurt?" asked Andrew looking at Graham's lacerated knuckles.

"'Course it hurts," Graham snapped, wrapping his hanky around his swollen fingers.

Just then, Mr. Bugle, who lived in the town, wheeled his bicycle out through the gates, hopped on and pushed off home for lunch.

All of a sudden Graham jumped up and ran out into the middle of the road. Cupping his hands around his mouth, he yelled at the top of his lungs, "I HOPE YOU GET RUN OVER BY A BUS!"

"Crikey!" exclaimed Andrew. "Now you've done it!"

"Nah, he's out of earshot," shrugged Graham. Giving vent to his anger had made him feel a lot better. "Race you to the dining hall, Andy!"

They scrambled into their places just in time to enjoy Mrs. Mulligan's scrumptious shepherd's pie.

No sooner were they settled back in their classroom after lunch than Captain Flagg came through the door instead of Barney Google. His face was as stony as Stony Stratford.

Clearing his throat, the Captain said, "It is my sad duty to inform you . . ." Graham's heart skipped a beat ". . . that Mr. Bugle was hit by a bus on his way home on his bicycle."

Twenty-three boys let out a horrified gasp.

"Did he get killed?" asked Jamie Jones.

"No, but someone in this class apparently wished he did."

Graham felt his stomach fill with wind. He darted Andrew a fierce look. But Andy shook his head, no, he hadn't told.

"Who?" asked Brian Soble curiously.

Captain Flagg ignored him and turned his steely eyes

144

on Graham. "That makes thrice," he said. "My office at four o'clock." And he began the lesson.

As the afternoon ticked by Graham's fears grew steadily. He knew that "thrice" meant "three times, you're out!" and "out" meant Borstal. "I'm never going there," he thought fiercely. "Nobody can make me."

Halfway through the afternoon he raised his hand and asked to be excused.

"What for?" snapped the headmaster.

"For the toilet, sir," Graham said. And Walter Sprunt, who sat behind him, whispered, "Pee-eww!" and held his nose.

"Hurry there and hurry back," barked the Captain.

Graham hurried, but not to the lavatory. Instead he ran straight upstairs to the dormitory, pulled on his coat and cap and Wellingtons and got his bag of money out from under the mattress. Then he walked casually back down the stairs. He heard Mrs. Mulligan singing "My Wild Irish Rose" as she clattered pots and pans in the kitchen. But no one else was about, so he managed to slip unseen out the front door.

Then he set off at a run for the railway station.

He bought a one-way ticket, no questions asked, and sat on a bench to wait for the train and to count his money. The ticket had used up all his earnings, but he still had the one pound and sixpence from Christmas. A fortune if he was prudent, as Mother Button would say.

Fifteen minutes later he was on the train, looking out the window at the rolling hills and fresh-tilled fields and soft green trees of England in springtime.

Chapter 25

Searching Again

Sitting on a bench in the Underground, Graham spread out a map of London on his lap. With the stub of a pencil from his pocket he carefully crossed out all the places he'd been before. Then he drew a line to the places he hadn't been to yet.

He went from place to place by tube and bus, searching. He asked dozens of ladies if their name was Robbertson, and they all said no. In Trafalgar Square again, he found himself standing in front of a big grey building that he'd never noticed before. Carved above the massive doors in huge block letters were the words CANADA HOUSE.

"Coo!" he cried aloud. "Wouldn't I like to go to Canada someday. In summer though, because Malcolm Dray's uncle went over in winter and got lost in a blizzard and was never seen or heard from again."

He didn't know how long his search would take him, so he stretched his money as far as it would go by eating chips wrapped in newspaper from fish-and-chip stands and apples from fruit-carts, and sleeping in empty railway cars at night. He was glad he'd worn his Wellingtons because it had begun to rain and the London streets were full of puddles. He wished he'd worn his mackintosh, too, because the air was cold and damp.

The second day he had a strange experience. It was suppertime and he had been walking around for hours. He needed to go to the toilet but he couldn't find a public washroom. He was standing in front of the Marble Arch Tearoom and in desperation, he went in. A waitress in a crisp white apron and frilly cap asked him what he wanted.

"May I please use the Gents'?" he asked politely.

Drawing her red lips into a bow she looked him up and down. He gave her his most winning smile and she couldn't help smiling back. She glanced over her shoulder to see if anyone was watching. Then she leaned down and whispered in his ear, "The coast is clear," and pointed with her pencil to the back of the tearoom. "You'll be quick about it won't you?"

"Yes, Miss. Thank you, Miss."

He forced himself to walk casually so as not to draw attention to himself. The tearoom was warm and there was no draft in the hall, but as he made his way to the back shivers ran up and down his spine and the hair on the nape of his neck prickled.

He hurried as fast as he could, thanked the nice waitress and left the Marble Arch Tea Room. As soon as he was out on the street again the shivers went away. Then he remembered what Mother Button used to say about that crawly, cold feeling: "Someone just walked over my grave," she'd whisper.

By nine-o'clock that night he was so tired he nearly went to sleep leaning on a lamppost.

Rubbing his eyes and blinking to stay awake, he saw a light glowing in the window of a small hotel across the street. A woman looked out the window, then drew the curtains, and the light disappeared. The woman reminded him of someone. Who was it? Oh, yes, he remembered now, it was Mrs. Temple, the lady who had come to his rescue in Leicester Square when he had been attacked by the gang of hooligans. And hadn't she invited him to visit the next time he was in London?

He remembered her address: Number 47 Aston Road, Bayswater. Matthew was right, he did have a photographic memory. He found Bayswater on the map and hopped on a bus.

"Will you please tell me when we get to Aston Road?" he asked the clippie as she took his fare.

"Right you are." She cranked out his ticket and handed it to him. "But you should be home in bed, a young lad like you."

He nearly said, "None of your silly business," but he bit his tongue just in time and gave her a friendly smile instead.

Alighting from the bus at Aston Road he hurried through the puddles along the footpath to number 47. It was a two-storey red-brick house with lights glowing in the bay window. He leapt up the wide front steps and rang the doorbell. It chimed inside like Big Ben.

In a moment the curtain on the door's window moved and Mrs. Temple's face peered out.

"What is it you want?" she called.

"It's me, Mrs. Temple, Graham Robbertson," he

cried. "Don't you remember me from Leicester Square?"

Instantly she opened the door and held out her hands. "But of course, I remember. Come in, come in, and tell me what you're doing out on this nasty night in London."

Pulling off his Wellingtons, he set them on a boot tray in the hall. Then he followed Mrs. Temple into a sitting room where orange flames crackled in a stone fireplace. Besides the firelight, the room was softly lit by shaded lamps on little tables. Never in his life had he felt so close to being home.

"Take off your wet things," she said, "and hang them over the chair-back in front of the fire. I'll go make us some tea."

Chapter 27

Confessions

With a warm cup of tea in his hands and his sock feet toasting in front of the fire, Graham told Mrs. Temple everything he had been up to.

"I got brought up in front of the magistrate and nearly got sent to Borstal," he confessed.

"Oh, my!" Mrs. Temple's hand went to her throat. "I've heard about Borstal. It's quite notorious. I'm glad you didn't go there."

"I would have, but my teacher, Miss Featherstone — she's ever so nice, and pretty, too — she spoke up for me and that's when the magistrate said he'd give me one more chance. So he sent me to Captain Flagg's School for Homeless Boys in Stony Stratford."

He told her all about Greystone and how he kept getting into scrapes by accident. Then he confessed what he'd yelled at Mr. Bugle.

"But don't worry, he didn't get killed," Graham assured her. "He must have been all right because he snitched on me. Then Captain Flagg said, 'That makes thrice.' Thrice means 'Three times and you're out.' I'm not afraid of a caning, but I am afraid of Borstal. So I left."

"I'm sure the accident wasn't your fault, Graham, but . . . tell me . . ." Mrs. Temple picked up his steaming coat from the chair by the fire, turned it inside out, and hung it back on the chair. "Why do you run off like that?"

"I'm looking for my mother," he explained. "I'm sure she's somewhere here in London because my birth certificate says that's where I was born." He told her in detail, then, about all his adventures in London.

"I searched in Ipswich, too, because my mate, Matthew, had relations there and he thought maybe I was looking in the wrong city."

"Where's your mate, now?" asked Mrs. Temple.

"He's dead. So I don't have a mate no more."

They were silent for a while, sipping their tea. Then Mrs. Temple spoke. "Well, Graham, there's only one thing to do. You must call the school and let them know where you are." Fear flashed across his face and she added quickly, "You'll be in much worse trouble if you don't."

"I don't know the number," he whispered.

"I can get it from Directory Inquiries," she said. "I can call for you, if you like."

He was tempted. She would know just what to say . . . and maybe she could save him like Miss Featherstone had. But then he thought of Captain Flagg saying in his booming voice: "Stand up and be counted like a man."

"I have to do it myself," he said.

So Mrs. Temple placed the call and handed him the phone.

He stayed overnight at 47 Aston Road. "It's my daughter Portia's room," Mrs. Temple explained as she led him up the stairs. "But she's away right now at Nottingham University. She's studying to be an archaeologist like her father."

It was the first time she'd mentioned her family. "Where's Mr. Temple, then?" he asked.

"He was killed ten years ago during an expedition in Australia," she said. "Mortimer was a born adventurer." She sighed, and he knew not to ask any more questions.

Graham would never forget that night; it was the first time he'd ever had a bedroom to himself. It was a lovely bedroom, though girlish, of course. Portia's graduation picture was in a silver frame on the dressing table. She was pretty, like her mother. "If Mrs. Temple was my mother," he thought, "Portia would be my big sister." He sighed and went to sleep under the eiderdown, pretending that it was true.

The next morning Mrs. Temple woke him early, fed him a hearty breakfast of eggs and sausages, and took him to the nearest railway station. She bought him a ticket to Stony Stratford.

"Promise me you'll go straight back and take what comes?" she said smoothing down the tuft of hair on the crown of his head.

"I promise," he said, and climbed onto the puffing train . . .

Captain Flagg was waiting for him on the platform at Stony Stratford. Not a word was spoken as they walked back to Greystone. Graham glanced at him out of the corner of his eye. The headmaster's expression was inscrutable.

When they arrived at the school, Graham saw that the arched front windows were crowded with boys' faces. Throwing back his shoulders and sticking out his chin, he followed Captain Flagg in the front door and down the long hall to his office.

Without being told, Graham dropped his trousers, leaned over the back of a chair and hid his face in his arms. Six whacks of the cane landed on his bare behind. They stung, but Graham had the notion that Captain Flagg was not putting all his weight behind the whacks.

Borstal was never mentioned, and Graham never ran away again.

Chapter 28

Never Give Up

As Graham got older, life became more complicated. He worked harder at his studies, and as one of the older boys at Greystone, he was given more responsibilities. Yet he never gave up his quest to find his mother. Everywhere he went he kept a sharp lookout.

He finished his schooling at Greystone when he was sixteen. Then he was on his own. He didn't quite know what to do with himself so he decided to go back to Bury St. Edmunds and talk it over with Mother Button. After all, Velma Villa was the only home he'd ever known, and Mother Button was the only mother he'd ever had.

Mother Button had hardly changed at all, except that her hair was a little greyer and she'd grown a little stouter. But poor Auntie Murna was so stooped over now that she could only look at the floor. Mother Button had hired a strapping big woman by the name of Elsie Stromberg to help her with the boys.

Flossie still lived nearby with her husband, Adam Hook, and her two little girls, Patricia and Lillian. She came rushing over to Velma Villa as soon as she heard that Graham had come home. The minute she saw him she threw her arms around him and gave him a big hug, and a kiss that made him blush. "My, you've grown to be a handsome young man, Graham," she cried.

"Well, you haven't changed a bit, Floss, you're as pretty as ever," Graham managed to say.

Then they all sat down around the familiar oval table for tea. "Have you got a job yet, Graham, now that you've finished school?" asked Flossie.

"Not yet, Floss. I don't know where to start looking."

"Well, my Adam needs help at the greengrocery. How would you like to start there?"

As a boy at Velma Villa, Graham's favourite chore had always been a trip to town with Mother Button to fill the pram with fresh goods from the greengrocer's. He loved the smell of the fresh fruits and vegetables and flowers.

"I think I'd like that, Floss," he said.

So he started at the greengrocers the very next day.

Over the next five years, Adam Hook taught Graham the business from the ground up. When he was twenty-one, he got up the nerve to go into Barclays Bank and ask for a loan. To his astonishment, he got it. Then he opened up his own small shop on St. Helen's Street in Ipswich. He had a green canvas awning made for across the front of his shop, with lettering that read: "Robbertson's Greengrocer, Fruiterer and Florist." Standing on the sidewalk to admire it, he thought, "I wish my mum was here beside me now."

By the time he was thirty-six years old Graham had become a successful and respected businessman in Ipswich. When asked, he gave much of the credit to

Mother Button, who had taught him manners and morals, and to Captain Flagg, for teaching him fair play and honesty.

He fell in love and married Jean Plum, and they had a son, Martin, and a daughter, Susan. He had a family and a future any man could be proud of. But still it bothered him that he had no past: no grandparents nor ancestors nor heritage to pass down to his children. Graham had not given up his quest. For ten years, once a month without fail, he put an advert in the personal column of the *London Times*. The rest of the month, he tried not to think about it.

Then one day he came home from work and his wife handed him a letter. It was postmarked Toronto, Canada.

Puzzled, he opened it and began to read. His heart quickened, and he read it aloud, breathlessly, to Jean.

Dear Mister Robbertson,

You don't know me, but I have a friend in England who sends me the London Times *because she knows I like to keep track of the Royals. I was born in England and was brought to Canada when I was a little girl. Well, one night when I couldn't sleep I got up and made myself a cup of tea and began leafing through the paper. When I came to the "personals" I read them out of idle curiosity. But when I spotted yours I did a double take. The surname Robbertson leapt out at me. It was my maiden name, you see, and I've never known another person who spelled it that way. So I felt compelled to send you this letter. If you are at all interested please write to me at the above address.*

Sincerely,
Sarah Robbertson Baxter

Graham sat at the kitchen table, stunned. Jean handed him a writing-pad and fountain pen, but ten minutes later he hadn't moved a muscle.

"What's the matter?" asked Jean.

"I'm afraid of another disappointment," Graham said with a sigh.

"You've lived through hundreds of disappointments," Jean said. "One more won't kill you. Write."

Graham smiled, and wrote:

Dear Sarah,

I received your letter today and was taken aback. You are quite right, the name Robbertson with two b's is rare indeed. I know because I have searched through just about every directory in England.

Let me tell you a little about myself. I was brought up an orphan boy. At three weeks of age I was left by my mother at the Home for Unwanteds in London. I have my birth certificate with my name and my mother's name on it. My mother's name was Marietta Robbertson. Does that mean anything to you? If so I would be obliged if you would reply.

Yours truly,
Neill Graham Robbertson.

Sarah's answer arrived ten days later.

Dear Graham,

I received your most welcome letter. I am almost afraid to put this into words, but I must. I think you may be my brother. Your mother's name and my mother's name are the same. But there is so much more to the story. If I could afford to I would come to England to meet you. But I cannot. Is there any chance you could come here? I will look forward eagerly to your reply.

Kindest regards from
Sarah Robbertson Baxter.

"Go!" said Graham's family.

Chapter 29

The Quest Ends

At Malton Airport in Toronto, Graham stood with his back against a wall anxiously scanning the crowd. Suddenly, through a sea of faces, he saw a woman who looked familiar: she was the image of his mother that he had carried in his mind all these years. Beside her, clinging to her hand, was a boy about six years old.

"Cor blimey!" exclaimed Graham breathlessly. "He looks just like me!"

They greeted each other shyly. When Graham bent to shake the boy's small hand, he heard a soft toot.

Sarah laughed nervously. "It's past his lunchtime, and he always does that when he's hungry," she said.

Graham burst out laughing, and everyone's shyness melted away.

* * *

That night, after young Damien had been tucked up in bed and Sarah's husband, Daniel Baxter, had gone off to work on the night shift, Graham and Sarah sat side by side on the living room couch. On the coffee table in front of them was a brown leatherette family album and a note pad.

Sarah opened the album. On the first page was a portrait of a bride and groom and under it, in white ink on the black paper, was written, "Marietta Robbertson and Frank Webster on their wedding day: June 2, 1942."

"My seventh birthday," Graham murmured.

His mother looked exactly as he had imagined all those years: a stocky young woman in a white dress and feathered hat; in her right hand she held a bouquet of flowers. Her left hand was tucked in the crook of her husband's arm. He stood proudly beside her in the uniform of the R.C.A.F., his peaked cap tilted over his right eye.

The next picture was of little Sarah sitting on a big wicker chair.

"You look the image of my daughter, Susan," he told her.

"And Damien looks just like you, Graham," she said. "Aren't family resemblances amazing?"

"Amazing," he agreed. "You could even say miraculous."

She smiled and turned page after page. Finally they returned to the first page: his mother as she must have looked when she had abandoned him.

"Now tell me the rest of the story," Graham said.

Sarah reached for the notebook. "I wrote everything down so I wouldn't forget a word," she said. She began to read.

June 14, 1971. Three days ago my mother, Marietta Robbertson Webster, died of cancer. The day before she passed away she said she had a secret that she couldn't take with her. And this is what she told me, word for word: "Sarah, you have a brother. His name is Neill Graham Robbertson. The day your father deserted us without a penny was the day Neill Graham was born. I had a part-time job waiting for me at the Marble Arch Tea Room but—"

Graham gasped and put his hand to his mouth. "What is it?" Sarah whispered.

He shook his head, leaned back and closed his eyes. "Keep reading," he said.

". . . I had a part-time job waiting for me at the Marble Arch Tea Room but I knew I couldn't earn enough money there to take proper care of two young children. So I did the only thing I could think of . . ." Here mother faltered and I wiped away her tears and begged her to stop talking and rest. But she went on, ". . . I gave my baby boy to the Home for Unwanted Children in London. But he wasn't unwanted. I just didn't know what else to do. I was only twenty-one, you see, and had no other family. I was beside myself with worry. Then I left England and worked my way to Canada as a nanny for the children on shipboard. One of the ladies, who liked my way with children, offered me a full-time job in Toronto. Seven years later I got an uncontested divorce and married your stepfather, Frank Webster."

Sarah squeezed Graham's hand and sighed deeply. "Perhaps you'd best stop for now," said Graham gently.

"No. I want you to hear it all."

Graham fetched her a glass of water, and she continued.

Mother could barely speak above a whisper now, but she went on. "After our marriage, Frank encouraged me to write to the Home for Unwanteds in London. I did and at last I got a letter back telling me that the Home had been levelled in the Blitz and the records had been moved for safekeeping. All they could tell me was that Neill Graham had been placed and it was against the rules to tell me where . . ."

Sarah sighed and closed the notebook. "Mother fell asleep then and she never woke up again. I wrote all this down after the funeral, so I wouldn't forget a word. Then I locked the notebook away and I never looked at it again until I read that ad in the *Times*."

They sat quietly for a moment, not speaking. Then Sarah said, "What about the Marble Arch Tea Room, Graham?"

Graham told her what had happened that day in London, so many years ago. As he spoke, the back of his neck began to prickle. He rubbed it and shook his head. "It was like a premonition," he said. "I never forgot it, and now I know why."

"Well, I guess I know why I couldn't sleep the day I read your ad in the personals. It wasn't a premonition, it was a miracle. I knew right away you must be my brother."

They laughed and hugged each other. Then they talked for hours, wanting to know everything there was to know about each other.

162

That night Graham lay on his sister's pull-out couch in the living room, his hands clasped behind his head, almost afraid to go to sleep for fear it was all a dream. His mind teemed with memories, then one stuck out above the rest: Christmas at Greystone, sitting alone in the dormitory with Andrew Noble-Gresty, feeling sorry for themselves.

"Never you mind, lads!" Captain Flagg's big voice came booming across the years. "Someday it will all be made up to you. Mark my words!"

Another voice followed: Miss Featherstone's, clear and sweet: "I am the boy's teacher and I can vouch for his honesty."

And finally, a third voice, soft as the summer breeze whispering in the window.

"Never give up, mate!"

Graham smiled. "I never did, Matty!"

BERNICE THURMAN HUNTER was a storyteller from an early age, but it was not until her children were grown that she began to get her work published. Now she is one of Canada's favourite writers of historical fiction for children, with a dozen books to her credit, including the best-selling *Booky* and *Margaret* trilogies, *Lamplighter, Janey's Choice* and *Two Much Alike*. Bernice has also earned many awards: *Amy's Promise* won the 1997 Red Cedar Award, and in 1989 Bernice was honoured with the Vicky Metcalf Award for her contribution to Canadian children's literature.